The Seduction

THE Seduction

a novel

Sara Torres

TRANSLATED BY
Mara Faye Lethem

PRIMERO
SUEÑO PRESS

ATRIA

*New York Amsterdam/Antwerp London
Toronto Sydney/Melbourne New Delhi*

PRIMERO SUEÑO PRESS

ATRIA

An Imprint of Simon & Schuster, LLC
1230 Avenue of the Americas
New York, NY 10020

First Primero Sueño Press/Atria Paperback edition June 2026

PRIMERO SUEÑO PRESS / ATRIA PAPERBACK and colophon are registered trademarks of Simon & Schuster, LLC

Simon & Schuster strongly believes in freedom of expression and stands against censorship in all its forms. For more information, visit BooksBelong.com.

For information about special discounts for bulk purchases, please contact Simon & Schuster Special Sales at 1-866-506-1949 or business@simonandschuster.com.

The Simon & Schuster Speakers Bureau can bring authors to your live event. For more information or to book an event, contact the Simon & Schuster Speakers Bureau at 1-866-248-3049 or visit our website at www.simonspeakers.com.

Interior design by Esther Paradelo

Manufactured in the United States of America

1 3 5 7 9 10 8 6 4 2

Library of Congress Cataloging-in-Publication Data has been applied for.

ISBN 978-1-6680-9298-9 (pbk)
ISBN 978-1-6680-9299-6 (ebook)

For us,
who one day navigated seduction sweetly
and tempered the damage

Infants begin to see by noticing the edges of things.
How do they know an edge is an edge?
By passionately wanting it not to be.

—ANNE CARSON, *Eros the Bittersweet: An Essay*

I perform, discreetly, lunatic chores;
I am the sole witness of my lunacy.
What love lays bare in me is *energy*.

—ROLAND BARTHES, *A Lover's Discourse: Fragments*, translated by Richard Howard

We desire fusion, but become aware of the abyss.

—MICHEL ONFRAY, *Théorie du corps amoureux. Pour une érotique solaire*

The Seduction

1.

My history of desire is basically a history of failure, everything I wanted and couldn't have, all the times I trembled in the distance that separated me from the object of my affection.

We don't sit across from each other in car number three of the train leaving the Estació de França on its way to the beach house. Our bodies are sitting at a diagonal. We avoid an intimacy that could easily be shared with a stranger. She sits by the window, traveling backward. I am on the other side of the table, with one foot escaping toward the gray floor of the aisle.

If touching her were possible, I would know what to do. I would know exactly what to do.

In songs, it's never a woman boasting about being able to rock another woman's body, leaving her shocked and trembling. But I know what I'm capable of. What's the point of false humility or innocence? My claim isn't born of arrogance or some lust for power. It's just fair.

There's an empty seat beside her thigh, where she rests the bag with her laptop and some books she never starts reading. I observe her. She surveys the landscape. A succession of white houses and pine trees. Dry earth and the tall plumes of my favorite plant ever since I was a girl, pampas grass: a proud, resilient species that makes roadsides more beautiful and is stigmatized with the label "invasive."

Now I pretend to also be enjoying the landscape. What seems relevant to her doesn't matter to me, and my slight nervousness won't let me hide it. My eyes return to her body with raw curiosity. I see a white knit vest with a V-neck, her bare shoulders peeking out. Moles and pale spots travel down her arm until they find the scar, a puncture mark on her skin, the small irruption of a vaccine that indicates a generational gap. I grew up looking at my mother's. I don't have one.

I've come this far, drawn by a photograph on the cover of a book titled *Pleasure and Time*. In that portrait, a woman who was not yet herself seemed absent as the camera chose her among all other things. She was its focus, behind her the vague branches of a bush and the last afternoon light on . . . the sea? The composition was of shadows, her hair falling on her shoulders and back. Her face in profile, with raised forehead and lightly pursed lips—a serious expression, firm and relaxed at the same time. Barely a lick of light touching her temple, the line of her nose, mouth, chin.

On the new release table at a bookstore in the Raval neighborhood, a portrait taken at dusk of a body perhaps sleepy from the sun and sea or, who knows, maybe happy after a day at the beach that stretched out into the night. Into the night because the desire in the gaze of the one taking the photograph is evident, vivid. That was what lured me in: understanding the gaze that portrays a face yet urgently captures something going on a bit farther down, in her torso covered by a white short-sleeved T-shirt. Its folds revealing every interaction of the fabric with the flesh beneath.

Those were perhaps the final hours of a summer night, sticky with salt and slightly colder. Pleasure and time, the curve of her bare breast and darker nipple brushing the cloth, its tautness creating waves. I thought that, if it were possible for me to touch that body, I would know what to do; I would know exactly what to do.

And I took the portrait with the novel attached to it. I brought it to my room; I looked at it for several days before deciding to read it. The text was secondary.

Once I was told there was something in the movement of my pupils, capricious and independent of each other, that made my gaze different from the way eyes are supposed to focus on the world. Now, when I find the same trait in her—honey-colored eyes slanting downward, inquisitive and sad, losing their symmetry—I feel I understand, for the first time, the power of a different gaze.

She doesn't direct it toward me during most of the trip. Is she avoiding me? Is she observing me out of the corner of her eye, not facing me, so she won't have to start a conversation? Her interest flees toward the window, toward the monotonous passage of alternating fields of crops and small solitary homes.

On the surface of the glass, I see her reflection—chestnut-brown hair falling in waves onto her narrow shoulders, her thin arms resting on her knees. Every once in a while, as if in conflict with a thought, she furrows her mouth in a small spasm or tightens her right hand that holds the leash.

She still hasn't spoken its name. When she notified me she'd be coming, she wrote: *My dog will come with us, too; she loves the sand and playing amid the tall grasses around the house. She doesn't let strangers touch her*. Was I the stranger?

Swaying with the train's clatter, the animal rests its head on a cloth fish it sometimes licks ceremoniously, as if to calm itself. At one point it picks the toy up in its mouth and tosses it toward the aisle. My travel companion lengthens one long arm over the empty seat and, since she still can't reach it, extends her entire body, folding at the waist, and finally rescues the saliva-damp cloth with the tips of her fingers.

I could take her photograph now. In a way, I am, but the image won't remain intact in my mind. I don't know when there'll be sufficient intimacy for me to be able to pull out my camera and place it between us. A lens to advance into her space. To intercede. Despite the attitude that imposes a distance, there are barely a few centimeters separating her legs from mine. If I took a photo now, it would almost be violent.

Nevertheless, she had said: *You can take photographs; it's a good location*. She spoke of the light at seven in the evening. All this to formalize an invitation in reply to an email of mine asking if

I could photograph her in the home where she would write her next novel. My project was a collective book of portraits of female authors and artists working. She accepted tersely and then didn't bring up the subject again. In our later communication, she talked a lot about the house, about its various rooms and what she referred to as *the principles of coexistence*, a series of notes about plans for mornings and evenings, according to the sun's rhythm. When she saw me arrive at the station loaded down, she pointed quizzically at the black bag I carried in addition to my suitcase. "This is my camera . . ." I said optimistically, as if that were something we both wanted. She didn't respond. She turned away. She lifted her shoulder bag a few centimeters above her low-heeled shoes and shortened the dog's leash as she headed to the open door of car number three. I walked behind them, like a girl, without being one, or only just a little.

There's nothing special about the Altafulla station. The train stops as if in a void between two more popular destinations. She points to the top part of a metal fence, where there's a sign with a phone number below the word TAXI.

"We won't call. They won't come. Tourism. Is your suitcase very heavy? Even if they did pick up the phone, we'd have to wait too long. And this isn't a pleasant place to wait."

My suitcase is pretty heavy. I vigorously shake my head no.

I lie twice. No. No.

Later I'll have to bear the excessive weight of baggage planned for an indefinite period of time, with inexact plans.

◆ ◆ ◆ ◆

Thursday, six thirty in the evening. September. Uphill, dampness and heat in a cloudy sky. Across the road, a bright-red house with a farm-type fence in the same color. Pizzeria La Trattoria. Closed doors, empty outdoor seating, and a menu at the entrance with all the prices crossed out in pen. Two stone lions with open mouths in the garden.

"We're fifteen minutes away."

We pass several streets of stone houses, some with brick arches surrounding large wooden doors. We stop for a second in front of one with a tiny store on the street level. There is a sign with an outline of a witch that reads PASTISSERIA ÀNGELS. She hesitates, wishes the baker a good afternoon. She says, "I'm thinking it'd be better if I come back tomorrow morning first thing."

This woman lives in this place. As well as on the cover of the book that spent so many days on my bedside table. Now I walk beside her. I wish someone would see me and remember us some years later.

2.

The front door is hard to open. Metallic friction and pushing until the handle hits a stone wall. The door is blue, and also salt residue and rust. From the first moment, I adopt a special attitude toward that door. I admire it, establish a relationship, become complicit with it. Before opening it, the writer has to twice turn a key hanging from a sailor's knot. Soon, I anticipate, one of these days, my hand will hold that braided cord . . . it will be my turn to push the key into the lock's slit. To confidently push the handle, which has been worn down to a paler blue. Some neighbor will see me and think: *Look, she's been sleeping there for several days, that guest.*

She first opens the door to the garden, then the main door, drops the bags, and walks to what I imagine will be the kitchen, all without saying a word. Without looking at me. Addressing only the dog, to whom she murmurs, "We made it. We're here."

I remain trapped in the doorframe. Doesn't she know that she has to invite me once more, right in that moment, so I can come in? What she wrote in the email isn't enough. Reality is now, and it needs renewed vows. Did she change her mind?

We don't know each other. In my first email, I could have been more sincere. I could have declared some things: that after reading her book I'd understood the part of the story she'd repressed, the part she held back. I could have told her that I knew the male character wasn't a man but rather a young woman with strong hands. I could have promised her things. A break from herself. A body fucked so long, with such calm and interest, that it finally forgets the world's demands. But, out of a fear of sounding arrogant, I was the first to keep silent. Like she is keeping silent now.

I was very happy planning this moment. In my daydreams I never imagined the worry, the fear of rejection. What am I supposed to do today if the awkwardness continues? Be patient. Pretend. Hide my disappointment to avoid conflict, and later, perhaps, with the suitcases opened and the clothes placed in the closet, I will cease to be invisible to her.

I've thought about this house a lot. It was in our conversations. Now I try to establish analogies between the place and the story of the place. Finally I find one, unquestionable, iconic: the old wooden shutters on the windows, hand-painted by her and a friend last summer in a tone similar to the doors on the blue streets of Chaouen. In other details of the house, reality also coincides with the mental image I'd created: The floors are worn and irregular, and Majorcan ikat fabric covers a large portion of the living room wall, the banner of some Mediterranean dream. An old pine table with a glazed clay vase, two green glasses, and four empty chairs. In the blue-and-white kitchen, a bunch of small flowers similar to wild chamomile. Everything is older and simpler than I'd imagined. The colors also seem deeper; the surfaces have the complex texture that develops over years.

She approaches the flowers and examines the inside of their vase. "They're thirsty, but first I'm going to change my shoes." She takes off her pumps and pulls some flat beige espadrilles with white stripes out of a basket. She strips her feet bare and changes into them just half a meter away from the floor tile where I am standing as if trapped on a checkerboard, unsure of my next move.

Then she looks at me; finally she looks at me. She smiles almost sweetly, with surprise.

"Make yourself at home, girl. Why are you still standing there? Do you want to borrow something more comfortable? There must be some hotel slippers stashed somewhere . . . Look, take these, they've barely been worn."

I am about to take off my shoes and socks in front of her, but I immediately dismiss the idea. I couldn't, not before first checking the state of my feet. I'm afraid for that to be the first nude part she sees of me.

Now she speaks. She leads me through the hallway carrying a mustard-colored towel, with a bar of honey soap in the middle, over her forearms. I receive the trousseau right by the door.

A little while later, alone in my assigned room, I will google her age.

Fifty years old. I'm thirty-two.

◆ ◆ ◆ ◆

I'd done that before—put her name into the search engine and waited a few seconds. I'd done it many times in recent months, although I hadn't remembered her exact age. Her Instagram account offers very limited information: a dozen posts over the span of three years. Pictures from a few talks and book launches. A photograph of the blue door and also the image that is on the cover of her book. That was my best discovery: the clean photograph, without the title and logos of the cover.

In another image, a finger caresses a bumblebee nestled in the palm of her hand. I think it must be dead. Bumblebees don't usually like being caressed that way.

The first time I enter what will be my bedroom, the dog goes through the door that has been opened for me before I do. Then it sits in the middle of the room, observing me with a chocolate gaze neither tender nor hard, its body neither tense nor relaxed, just attentive in some sort of perfect dose of discernment. It is a tall animal, like the writer, with somewhat odd proportions and a lot of fur of an irregular color; it seems like the unexpected offspring of a greyhound and a sheepdog. I don't attempt to approach or pet it. Its position makes clear this is not the right moment.

"Let's see how you like it here. This is usually the room where Greta stays, but she won't arrive for another few days. Don't be frightened by the walls—I tore off the old paper and underneath there was this green, such a lovely pigment. Although, of course, ruined by glue and time. I asked them to leave it just as it was and apply a fixative. Now it's like sleeping against the wall of a hotel in ruins in an Italian city."

She brings up ruins, but there is no need. It's unlikely one could be in here and not think of a nostalgic link with some hazy past. *What hotel? What Italian city?* I feel like asking. Probably none in particular—just an impression, a vague idea, almost a mood.

The room has two spaces, connected by an arch. In the first is the bed, and in the smaller space, a low corner sofa, a dressing table, and a wooden platform; there's nothing on top of it.

"It's for the bathtub—you see those two holes? It's all set up for the water line, but I haven't chosen a model yet. Some people would buy one on the internet, without ever seeing it in real life. I'd like to try it out first, but where do you go to try out bathtubs, do you know?"

I shake my head. I find it amusing to imagine her with her long cotton dress and her lovely calves, wearing espadrilles with wedge heels, leaping into bathtubs in a display space—a large warehouse inside an industrial park.

A display space . . . as cold and different from a home as an internet gallery, I will mumble.

The dog leaves the room first but isn't the one to initiate the movement. The canine was watching the writer's face, which turned for a second toward the door. It wasn't a command; it was the unconscious expression of a desire. Which the dog understood: *Come on, let's get out of here.*

◆ ◆ ◆ ◆

I am left alone for the first time. I wait in the shiny green with its worn patches of torn paper. The sun is close to the horizon. Everything preserves the past, even the new: a radio that can't be connected to a cell phone so it can be used as a speaker. The doors are small and the furniture low, so the ceiling seems very far away from them. Sitting on the edge of the bed, I take a profile picture with the front camera of my phone, extending my arm and pretending my gaze is busy with some activity that has nothing to do with the camera. I want to know what she would see if she walked in now.

First, I check my eyes, which are almost always irritated, assessing the red around the irises that usually gets worse in the heat, in dry environments, and in moments of tension when I don't blink much. A gaze the color of that chestnut floor, so often crowned by tiny rivulets of blood. A brown and red path to offer other women.

My dark hair, my firm jaw, and my shirt buttoned up all the way to the neck. I remember, as a teenager, the irony of my mother saying that everyone respected the seasons except for me, for whom summer clothes didn't exist, since I was always "covered up to my eyebrows." My beautiful mother, unapologetically revealing the definition of her bare arm and her leg peeking out through the slit in her dress. A mother's athletic body as reference, and then my awkward transition between winter and summer, the obligatoriness of exposure.

All of that was violent. The change of seasons happened

without warning, and I couldn't strip off my clothes. Every woman around me had the promise of summer in mind. They seemed prepared; however, I was still the same in the heat of June as in December: an animal voraciously scarfing down what's placed in front of her, a languid, yellow piece of meat, sown with pores and dark hairs. The olive-and-black field of a teenager more concerned with obtaining pleasure by looking at other women than in maintaining an improbable norm in her own body.

For others it seemed easy, light. Stuffing thighs into stretchy elastane jeans. Waking up earlier to scrub their hair every day, apply a masque, dry and iron. Marking their eyelids with various tones of shadow. Combing their eyebrows and curling their lashes. Sticking contact lenses into their eyes and managing to produce enough tears throughout the day to keep their eyeballs from not turning into grapes in the desert.

I would observe them and their gestures that, when imagined in my own flesh, hurt me. But on them it all seemed painless and natural, their soft and beardless nature, their scent of raspberries and bananas. I suspected there was something acrid in my own smell, but I couldn't stand the chemical scent of deodorant clinging to my underarms all day. It was the expected smell, but once applied, its opacity annulled all the nuances of the skin and even the landscape. Not only the sweat smelled of deodorant, but so did the clothes, the atmosphere, and even the food.

Being able to stay in for several days, not go out on the street, was a rest from that smell and from other people's gazes. Confusedly and in private, I preferred the sour and the bitter; when

I was alone, I felt satisfaction with the reverberations of my sex and the gentle oil of my scalp.

Since I entered this house, my adolescent nervousness has returned, a discomfort in my own flesh that gains territory over the other, calmer, more independent version of myself that I was able to access after leaving high school and entering university.

Slimming down was the trick for everything. Every time I was attracted to a girl I would stop eating. Lose weight not to attract, but to avoid provoking rejection. It's the secret story of someone who now presents as confident, who knows the gestures of privileged bodies and repeats them, pretending. She spends so much time pretending that sometimes she forgets her true self: that insistent and ambitious deformity that has yet to find the way to silence its hunger.

Who am I now in this room, wondering about my scent, about my breath, the way the fabric of my pants draws a curvy hip instead of a straight leg?

During my adolescence I would go alone to the first beach day. Taking off my clothes was like unwrapping a large trembling mass that could overflow and change its volume many times. I sunbathed by myself for hours, on that first day and all the following ones. The heat seemed to dry out the texture of that mass and make it more tangible, with precise boundaries. In the sun my surface contracted and set. A prickly pear with irritated eyes. I would get very tanned, and in my dark skin I felt less fear of my flaccid flesh multiplying, revealing dimples and cracks. Later, toward the end of the summer, once I'd achieved the dark brown skin that hid details, I could join the other girls without fear of flattening them or horrifying them with my lack of definition.

In those days I could feel my boundaries shifting in every mirror; my body never seemed to be the same. I was constantly shocked. When I felt anxious for having suddenly widened, I learned to lift up my clothes and focus my gaze right on my navel, a somewhat stable point of reference. I had to look at it for three seconds, no more and no less, because after the fifth second, my belly would start to expand and deform. Then it was important to look outside, to carefully study the outline of a tree, a tile, a streetlamp.

Today, when I feel anxiety approaching, I use an old trick: I pick up my camera; I focus; I concentrate on the surroundings.

I'm sitting on the edge of the bed. I feel the weight of a terry cloth towel on my knees. This space fits into the category of "bedroom without a bathtub." A room organized around an absence at its center, whose presence determines everything: the mood, the layout of the rest of the furniture. But the water does not yet reach here. A couple of holes in a flaking wall.

The absence of a bathtub thwarts the pleasure of two women bathing together. The bedroom could enable such bliss. Somehow it announces an abundance yet fails to complete the gesture.

To the right of the bed hangs a small illustration, a copy of some ancient codex. A woman riding on a seven-headed dragon, wearing a feather headdress and lifting a chalice in one hand. Beneath her is a title, *The Great Whore of Babylon*, followed by a small handwritten description:

> *Then one of the seven Angels who hold the seven bowls came and spoke with me, saying: "Come, I will show you the wisdom of the great harlot, who sits upon many waters. With her, the queens of the earth have lain. And those who inhabit the earth have been inebriated by the wine of her love."*

I've found an image to rest upon. A compassionate image. The heads of the dragon on which the Whore rides look like the writer's dog in profile: the bulging, open eye; the tongue hanging out with short, rapid panting. The sweetness of the writer as she looks at it, asking about its thirst.

A tiredness accumulated over days finds its path. I fall asleep for a few minutes, until I'm awakened by her voice calling me from the kitchen.

The kitchen is large enough for a square table with two chairs and a wooden stool. The hydraulic tile floor shows the blue-and-white checkerboard where I got trapped when I arrived. Now I cross it without asking for permission.

Our first supper takes place. In a large basket, a red-checked cloth covers a potato omelet resting on a porcelain plate. The spoils include two bread rolls and some paper napkins. She ordered it for our arrival from a nearby bar.

"Don't think this is how I usually eat. On a regular day, I'd have scrambled eggs and a bowl of soup."

I have to name the objects, look at them one by one and in relation to each other. The objects are important to her. They each have an individuality and a weight in the space. They are pretexts. They are there to hold gazes. The way she places them in the various rooms exerts a sort of attraction. It seems they act as dreamcatchers, sustaining and organizing ideas, serving as a sieve for the soul. Perhaps, once she's placed them in that ritual way, they protect her from bad thoughts. There are no bad thoughts possible in front of a soft, circular omelet caressed by checkered cloth. You cannot go into an anxious loop in front of bread rolls, a little pile of napkins. The number of objects gathered together is important. The mysterious proportion holds a spell.

She picks up a small knife to slice the spelt rolls in half and then uses it to cut a tomato that she pampers with olive oil and a few flakes of salt. "A simple supper," she says. "Cooking or writing, only sometimes both. When they happen on the same day, it's big news. It means one has succeeded at owning their time." But today she didn't write. Nor yesterday either. "There's a problem with time. Not just any sort will do; it has to be the kind that allows for special attention. Your arrival, for example, demands preparation, even though that isolated event wouldn't be a problem. It also contributes something. Then there are the small routine events, which draw one's attention toward a place where the thread of writing gets lost. Creative thought needs wandering, emptiness, even boredom. The world created itself on a bored day, yes, yes."

She says that people send her messages about all sorts of things. That her cell phone mercilessly sucks on the udder that is her life. She uses strong words, her thin wrist extended, without breaking the mood and without anyone around her getting their feathers ruffled.

With my cell phone, I try to record her hands placing the little knife on the table, the one she used to slice open the bread. She stops my action by waving the knife in front of my phone. It's an excessive, somewhat clumsy gesture that makes me laugh.

"Are you part of some anti-tech cult?" I ask without thinking and regret it immediately.

"No. But stop that."

It is said with gravity. Not anger. That balance is also curious.

I pounce on a bowl filled with olives that she places in the middle of the table. She doesn't touch them, and after a little while has passed, I decide to eat them two by two. Waiting to eat always causes an avalanche in me. I pile up the pits on a napkin, making sure they aren't visible from her seat, although I only partially succeed. I'm embarrassed by the gnawed pits, still marked with my saliva and urgency, resting on a shared object. I'm also embarrassed by the way the little pile becomes evidence of my voracity: If she were eating them, too, even just a couple, her hunger and mine would mix together in the remains. I wish I were able to stop before that self-portrait is completed.

I hear her talking about the house, my mouth full. I should know that the windows don't close well and the glass is very thin. I might need earplugs to sleep. The estimate for wooden windows was too expensive, and she still hasn't found a local carpenter willing to repair them. Adding a metal window to that space would be an unforgivable mistake.

It is a lot of work to maintain the interior of an old home, take care of it without erasing its character. It's a job that's equivalent to writing—contemplative, a task of composition. She says that one has to sit down in some corner, get their senses working, try to comprehend. Only after having comprehended with our senses should we intervene. The intervention responds to a need of the body in the physical and imaginary space.

She eats a slice of omelet with a piece of bread moistened with oil, splattered with salt. She adds two slices of tomato on top.

"What a boring conversation for someone who's just arrived, right? Predictable that I'd mention writing, when, really, I wanted to talk to you about what it means to finally have a house where I can sleep, eat, excrete, maintain a certain amount of calm. A place to land that isn't dependent on the love of others."

She pauses, delivering a silence unto me as if I should fill it. I have no idea how to continue; just a few seconds ago I was almost sure it was a monologue. I look into her eyes and decide to pour her a bit of water. I really like her. There's something in her face that makes me want to hold it in my hands and lick her mouth. Maybe I'm being influenced by the images in her book. The protagonist was someone whose mouth opened with pleasure, advancing her tongue slightly, leaving it relaxed against the inside of her lip. The protagonist sometimes enjoyed having people spit inside her mouth, just like that, as I'm now imagining her. What does *she* like? If she writes such scenes, they can't be completely foreign to her.

"After many years I've managed to arrive here, crouch down, leave my scent in the corners, and open up a friendly hollow to welcome others into. A house that depends only on my love."

Only on my love.

Sleep, eat, excrete, maintain a certain amount of calm.

Just like with the flaking paint on the walls, there is something decadent in the way she speaks. The words she chooses, her gravity. In another context I would think that what she's saying is dislocated, out of place, or desynchronized, out of step. But I am the one who entered her time and her space. I forced my way in, and I will have to adapt.

I imagine her words like a tumbledown boat: coral and green, moored to the entrance of a small port, bobbing up and down with the tides. I'm not used to people speaking in that way. If a friend did it, perhaps I would imitate her mockingly. Or let out a giggle.

But I don't want to laugh now. I prefer the opportunity to be someone else while I live in this place. I want to understand her. Not with my eyes, but with my listening. With my touch, when possible.

✦ ✦ ✦ ✦

The first night I will dream of a black horse coming very slowly into the bedroom. I will wake up at five thirty in the morning wanting to piss, and I will have reservations about leaving the bed and going into the bathroom, despite it being right next door. I will feel my way without turning on the lights, trying not to be noisy, but failing in my sleepy clumsiness.

The dog, surprised by my presence, will bark two clean barks from the writer's bedroom at the end of the hall.

I wake up with a strong smell of varnish that comes off the floor. The scent interfered with my rest because every muscle feels fatigue. Without thinking, I open up my inbox on my phone, searching for an email from her, like every morning before I arrived here. For a moment I imagined she would continue writing to me, understanding it as the path to more sincere communication.

She would usually begin her emails with *Good morning, beautiful*. Yet has her voice said anything similar since we met?

No. Nothing.

Not a single sweet word.

I'd heard her voice addressing me just once, days before I came. I was surprised because it sounded like in her recorded interviews, but not exactly. On the phone, as our conversation progressed, it seemed to go shriller, more childlike. Her voice in the distance was delicious. It gave me warmth and a surge, like salmon jumping upstream. *Come here*, its cadence and texture said to my body. There were no complex directions or spatial nuances offered; none of that mattered. "Here" was a concrete place close to both the belly and the mouth from which words flowed: She had called me; in other words, she had chosen me to speak to.

In person we still don't know how to think and lay our eyes on each other at the same time. It seems indiscreet to look at her directly, seek out her details, the pores of her skin, the intrusion of those gray, thicker hairs. Everything that doesn't form part of her public image.

I think about her voice on the phone and her way of looking at the dog as she offers it water. She crouches on the ground, puts her face at the level of the dog's snout, and places her hand around its jaw. The images begin to be very specific—an expression in her mouth when she speaks, a way of inquiring with her eyes about the animal's thirst. I cling to the images, trying to slow them down for a few seconds until they resume their movement, becoming a vague shadow. I don't turn on the light or allow the day to commence. I search beneath my pajama pants, in my panties, for a narrow corner where I can move my hand. The mouth offers water, says, "Come here." Now it is only the voice. I corner it against the wall; I lean on it; I squeeze it tight. It no longer speaks. It focuses on breathing. It breaks.

Yesterday, when she finished dinner, she went to bed early, and as she did, my stomach clenched. A contracting spasm. My stomach a fist a second before a woman disappears through the dining room door toward her rest.

The movement is similar to an inner spasm that seeks to contract time on the outside so the order of things reacts in favor of my desire. If my stomach closes up, perhaps I can manage to get something to stop in the rhythm of the real, yielding some extra time for her to change her mind. To come to me; add me to her route.

It was the first dinner, and she didn't drink even a single glass of wine. She offered me nothing more than a pitcher of ice water with lime, or a small bottle of Vichy mineral water as an alternative. Water and potato omelet. I can't stop thinking how that isn't the dinner you offer someone you are hoping to bed.

"Would you like an herbal tea?"

That was her last suggestion. More water. Water stained with plants. Dirty water.

Even sleeping alone, I would have needed a beer, some alcohol to relax my nerves from the arrival and possibly save myself from a long night of three hundred tosses and turns, and waking up parched at five thirty right in the middle of a dream.

The kitchen floor, its alternating white and blue, holds the morning light.

She went out to buy a loaf of walnut bread. She tells me that with her hair messy and in silk pajamas several sizes too large. She is wearing nearsighted glasses and sinks a teaspoon into a jar of pollen.

The belly of a spoon entering amid the yellow bits. Her slightly tan body among the silk. Her eyes distant and sleepy.

I feel the privilege of being able to look at her in her kitchen, on just another morning.

"Can I take your photo?"

"Of course not, thanks."

Something's wrong. Something's wrong? If I'm here in this house to take some portraits of her while she writes her next book, what am I supposed to do if I can't use my camera? And if I can't take photographs, and I can't take her either, how am I going to get her to recognize my worth? I don't trust I can win her affections merely by being here . . .

Other women, perhaps, win love just by occupying space. But that has never been my case. I've always had to work to gain access to others' passion . . . consciously step up onto a stage where suddenly my name makes an impact within a narrative that supports it. I've always known that just me, unpolished, wasn't enough. To reach where some women effortlessly reach, achieving true attention, I needed a feat, a constructed personality.

As a little girl, pointing an analog camera at my mother, I'd discovered something: My mother wanted to satisfy the lens as she'd never wanted to satisfy her daughter. With the camera between us, held in my hands, I had a power: the power of the gaze. Mamá positioned herself before me nervously, asking for advice, and then I was allowed to give her orders: *Lower your chin*; *hold the mug in your hands—a smile, but more relaxed*. With my face hidden behind the glass eye, for a few moments, I represented the power of judgment. She sucked in her belly and touched her hair. She searched for me time and again, needing me, needing confirmation: *Is this good, what do you think, sweetie? How do I look?*

"Of course not, thanks."

Something in her politeness feels forced. Refusing and saying thanks. Yet it isn't a provocation or sarcasm. I look at her again, arched forward; it seems she's hiding behind the arm that holds a cup of coffee. She covers her face.

Her face isn't perfect. Perhaps she doesn't know that it also wasn't perfect in the portraits of her I saw before I arrived. Her irregularity is not a surprise to me. She hides it. I desire it.

To shift away from the awkwardness, I tell her about my dream. A slow black horse, with no saddle strap or reins, not even a bridle, entered the bedroom, hoofs against the fired clay floor.

"I've seen something similar. A woman and a horse in an empty house, more crumbling and decaying than this one. It was a scene in a film called *Unicorn*. But the horse had no horn. That word has been used in many different ways, including as a designation for the third person in an erotic relationship, the person who seeks out the couple."

I stand to heat up a little more oat milk in the small saucepan.

Pushing the button, turning it to the left, and waiting for the sound of the gas is a nostalgic gesture. The burners, however, are newly installed. This is not her grandmother's stove, nor her mother's, nor the stove of other women's mothers or grandmothers.

"The person who seeks out the couple?"

"Yeah, the one who loves them both."

I'd like to ask her about her experiences, as if she were a friend. But her gravity prevents me.

She moves calmly through the different spaces inside the house, marking her territory. The kitchen is separated from the large living room by a wall, but it has no door. The living room has four windows that overlook the garden. Every time she moves an object, she repositions it in a specific way.

This woman is also the one who, a few months ago, responded in the affirmative to a girl who wrote to her on social media: *I want to meet you. Is that possible?*

She took charge, head-on. She didn't avoid the message the way she now averts her gaze. She began a conversation and, later, in an email, one morning at eight thirty, right after waking, she wrote: *It could happen in my house, the second week of September*.

She informs me of today's plans. Of the free and voluntary nature of the day's plans. She prepares two large baskets. Before the beach, we have to stop by the market. I can decide: go with her or stay.

The market is a structure hidden between other stone houses. To get there we cross the church square, at the foot of the castle.

Is she happy now? She seems to be. From the outside, I see a pleasant person, very careful not to make others uncomfortable. She smiles and says good morning in every stand we stop at. She asks for things, and the shopkeepers, after weighing her tomatoes, mushrooms, and cheese, come over to place them directly into our baskets—they grow heavy. She allows those bodies to approach; she appreciates the gesture, considers it natural.

Every so often she turns toward me and asks, "Do you like this? Is there something more you'd like?" Since I don't know how to respond, she insists. "You must have some preference." Then her worries return: "And the flowers, we can't forget the flowers."

They're sold by some old women in one corner of the market; they keep them in colorful buckets filled with water; they grow them in their gardens.

"Chamomile flowers for the kitchen and pink blush carnations for my bedroom. For yours . . . I still don't know which flower matches you best, but for the moment young eucalyptus leaves, in a clay vase, definitely."

"What about the flowers that were there when we arrived? How long have they been there?"

"Greta must have left them—she was staying at the house while I was working in Barcelona."

I want to ask who Greta is, but I don't feel able to. Something inscrutable in the way the writer expresses herself keeps me silent. I think that she herself should have explained their link, after dropping her name several times. *Greta, my partner. Greta, my best friend.* Her lover? Perhaps she would never say "Greta, my lover," because the phrase oozes sex and intimacy.

Greta, someone who sleeps alone in my room, in the empty house, and departs before we arrive. Who leaves us flowers. Who leaves them even knowing I am coming.

We put away the groceries and walk down along the Camí dels Munts toward the beach, coming across no one except a girl with long hair and a plaid jacket. She is walking a tiny black dachshund, who reacts when it passes the writer's dog. Even though the confused dachshund is on a leash, it launches into possessive barking.

The writer's dog is unleashed and, unfazed, turns its face away from the yipping, toward her knee, which peeks out beneath a white cotton dress with wide straps and covered buttons down the middle. The temperature is mild in the morning, much more so than in Barcelona, and a cool wind lifts as we draw closer to the coast. But I start to get uneasy under the direct impact of the sun. I stay glued to the cypresses, although they scarcely project any shade.

Her clothes are light, chosen to form part of the scene. My clothes, however, are like an eyesore in the photograph. I'm dressed in navy blue—slightly thick chino pants and a long-sleeved shirt. My shoes are closed and dark, gathering dust. Only my large rectangular sunglasses, with their heavy frames, protect me. Soon I break into a sweat; I feel the dampness in my armpits trapped beneath the fabric. If I stay here longer than a week, I'll need to find a solution for this. I'll go shopping at some point when she's busy.

There is something exhausting about first times. This anxiousness to control everything.

At the end of the road the sea appears, with little sparkling stars of light on its surface.

"That is the vision," she says. "How many times can we feel thrilled to see the Mediterranean at the end of a road? Every single time."

I shorten my steps to allow her to pass me, and when there's enough space between us, I take a photograph of the sea and of her facing away from me. I am carrying an old film camera—the roll doesn't advance automatically, and the sound of the shutter is almost imperceptible.

I comment that the beach is narrow in a way that's unsettling. She takes me to the broken facade of a house rooted in the sand; it's her favorite restaurant, Voramar. She says that only a year earlier it didn't look like this. The tide ripped off part of it, taking the front door and drowning the gardeners' agave plants in salt.

"Few people are attempting to include the material effects of climate change in their vision of the future. If everything changes as fast as that piece of the beach disappeared, if one day the tide carries off the spaces I remember, I won't be able to get used to it. I'm slow, you know? I like snails, hermit crabs. I like this sea because it doesn't have the northern currents; it's different from the dark Cantabrian Sea, where I was born. Now I can always swim calmly, doggy paddling with my head above the water. I hate to be rushed. I think I write so I don't have to rush around in the mornings to get to an office. I write so I don't have to go into an office, and so my work doesn't seem like work."

I tell her that one can be slow in photography, too, but you have to be still for a little while in front of the camera so the light can capture you.

"Are you trying to convince me of something?"

"No, I'm talking about the possibility of beauty in complicity. In allowing in the desire to depict intimacy."

"And when you have my portraits, who will you sell me to?"

"I'll use them to find you a husband. I'll send your photo to other countries and show you to potential spouses. Like in the movie *Portrait of a Lady on Fire*."

"Ha, ha, you know, I'm not sure that's a very good plan. What you have in front of you now, if you don't share it, is only yours. Don't you like that idea?"

Her image thrills me so much that I really couldn't bear it if my photographs were unable to reflect it. There is always the possibility that something fundamental will be snatched away forever. The static image sometimes reveals forms that are completely alien to a body in love.

Desire's gaze stares so much that it doesn't see. It suspends judgment because it penetrates through fantasy, what's been conjured up. Only with desire's gaze do I feel a complete aesthetic experience.

Hers is such a comfortable nudity, in low-cut panties. Very low, very far beneath her navel. It seems like she is waxed, but when I look closer, I see hair on her inner thighs. Fine blond hair; it's easy not to wax when it's like that.

We are emerging from the summer. The sun scorches the skin, but the ambient temperature isn't high. I think how I didn't even experience summer this year. I was at home, with the air on, in front of the computer. Drinking beer on the balcony at night with my small queer family. Some days we strolled through the countryside and went out by the river. We uncovered our bellies in a landscape with no strangers staring back at us. La Barceloneta in August was the after-hours spot for a hetero party. The calculated proportion of bodies could in no way represent the majority of mortals. The majority of mortals hide their thighs in an air-conditioned office, or wet them in rivers where they can relax in peace, play with their girlfriends.

But those of us on the margins always remember the norm. It's not something we'll suddenly one day forget. With or without guilty parties, there are always people, settings that remind us of it.

I don't really know what I think about the writer, what I was thinking when I went to get waxed before coming to meet her. The pain was moderate—it wasn't my first or second time. Even though I felt ridiculous when I looked at my bare armpits, I didn't have enough self-esteem to risk aversion over a detail that was under my control. It's true, that's how we nonconformists are: free. Free to assess when a tuft of hair under an arm weighs too much, takes up too much space. Free to remove it from the scene when planning an outing with an unknown woman. And free, above all, after flirting with the norm, to return home to our genderqueers. To hope that the hair grows back, accepting the advice to not get obsessed again with someone whose presence makes us anxious.

Look around you, I tell myself. *Forget your body and hers. Focus, for example, on the end of the beach, above which nestles Tamarit Castle. Focus on the small catamarans and on the catamaran dozing on the sand in front of the yacht club.*

Her legs are also covered in hair. The skin moisturized, calm. Mine, however, reddens with irritation from the salt entering the open pores. I struggle to find a position on the towel when I get out of the water. She, apparently calm, reads face down. Asses are magnificent in that position. Practically all of them, although probably not mine. When my anxiety over my body image increases, it's no longer possible for me to feel desire. Undoubtedly the fear provoked by my delusions of monstrosity wins out over the lovely image of her ass.

I know I'm being unfair. I feel like an idiot for having reduced her to some sort of prototype of femininity that makes me both anxious and desirous of having her near me.

✦ ✦ ✦ ✦

To keep from turning back into a teenager scared of her own flesh, I try to remember myself later, as a lover. Feeling desired for the first time broke the spell. Being in bed for the first time with a girl whom others also saw as the queen of the seven seas, as all the jade in Japan. Recognizing a hunger similar to mine in another's gaze, being immobilized by her advance toward me, by her search for me. I could understand that perhaps the feminine was just a stance in desire: waiting for the other to project a fantasy of curves and porosity, and then offering it to her. The feminine was nothing more than a welcoming attitude toward another's desire that elicits compassion, tenderness, craving.

Until I met her, capable of bending me and moving me, I had avoided any gesture that evoked femininity. I wanted to be appetite, gaze, and action. Never object. But I also enjoyed passivity. That was the discovery. An attentive, energetic passivity that was capable of transforming itself and transforming everything. Both of us passive and active, fucking and being fucked. I really miss the body I had back then. The satisfaction.

To be the object of someone's gaze in this world is to be exposed to the risk of awakening desire, repulsion, or rejection. If it is desire that we awaken, even if it gives us an immediate rush, isn't it too high a price to pay when its opposite lies in wait for us around every corner? The same gaze that chose us, a second earlier or a second later, can discard us with the same passion.

I could unveil myself on the sand, show my legs entirely, be completely exposed flesh in a single movement. Be relaxed in her line of sight, if she would just give me a sign, some small sign of tenderness.

Wasn't she the one who wrote it? Three sentences I underlined in her book:

> *Tenderness predisposes us to appreciate what is before our eyes. It suspends the laws of commerce; it is fascinated by the difference of what is most intimate to it. The beloved originates its own canon.*

I want more. To be chosen.

We waggle our shoes at the door to the house. We shake out the towels because no sand should come inside. Her concentrated face as she waves her arms is amusing. We shower at the same time, in two different bathrooms.

She suggests we go out to have a drink at some terrace. Says if I'm up for it, we can bring a book to read for a little while.

"To read together, sitting there?"

"Yes."

"I didn't bring any book I'm in the mood for now."

"Then you can choose one of mine."

She rests her hand on my back, between my shoulder blades, and gently leads me toward the bookshelf in the living room. A smell of baby powder and figs overtakes the upper part of my nose. The writer's push is subtle as I wait for the command to protract, become more complex, demand more.

"When you've read all of those, you can start in with the ones in my bedroom."

"In the photograph where you were caressing a bumblebee curled up in your palm, was it dead or dying?"

"It was alive and kicking. It spent a long time with me, and, after a very gradual approach, it allowed me to stroke it. Then I got distracted for a while. I thought it had left, but then I noticed a buzzing far too close, underneath my T-shirt. There it was! About to be crushed! I lifted up my shirt to set it free and it flew off."

"Didn't you think the bumblebee could have been your mother?"

"Normally my mother is a robin. She often used to appear in that tree, but it's been a long time."

"When my mother died, it occurred to me that she was the mosquitoes that buzzed in my bedroom at night. I heard that it's the female ones about to breed who bite us. Just in case they were Mamá, I let them take my blood. I haven't killed one since."

"You give yourself over to them."

"It's strange how we accept that need mothers have to drink our blood. It even seems fair."

"Perhaps it is fair. We remain too close for too long. We take too much from them, and later, when we are ready to leave, we abandon them with a voracious, bloody thirst."

"Mothers are very scary, aren't they?"

"Like passion after some time has passed. Any sort of passion. It's only not scary if it's fleeting."

We are both motherless daughters. Perhaps that is the common point she is searching for. What makes me interesting to her.

I've found breakfast set out on the kitchen table. A matching set of plate, silverware, and cloth napkin. A mug, a cup, and a pitcher of water with fresh mint leaves. There are blueberries, salt, an oil cruet, a small avocado. On her side of the table there's hardly anything: a bowl with a green stain on the bottom and the book *In Praise of Risk* by Anne Dufourmantelle. I've seen this book on various surfaces over the last few days.

The house is in silence, the door to her bedroom closed, and the dog is sunbathing in the garden, near the front entrance. The remains of tea seem to be a not-very-subliminal message for me not to wait for her.

I photograph the scene with a small Pentax I bought at Los Encantes, a flea market in Barcelona. The image will be soft due to the light coming in through the window.

I pick up the book and let it open at random on one page, then another, and another, page 91:

> *It is not easy to recover from the inner fragmentation that solitude can evoke when anxiety attacks the very possibility of our being in the world. [. . .] To enter familiarity with a certain solitude is to accept that supposedly reliable bonds are deceptive, and to take the risk of tarrying with yourself as an unknown friend, very gently, as you would enter into convalescence.*

I go out into the garden and continue reading on the grass, beside the dog. She accepts my company with no qualms, but if I extend my arm out toward her, she pulls her head away.

One hour, two, silence.

I go back to the bedroom for a while. Two hours more, three. I'm hungry and, when I go to the kitchen, I again find the table set: a soup plate and a pot with a stew of lentils, vegetables, and potatoes.

When did she cook?

I eat. I make time in the kitchen to see if we will coincide. I hear the door to the bathroom, the dog's paws moving through the hall, the door to the bedroom closing behind them. I wile away the day, accomplishing nothing.

I try to edit photos, but I have trouble concentrating. I'm alert, hoping something will happen. But what? A couple of words, a phrase with my name or a proposition.

It happens at dusk; we run into each other at a point halfway between her bedroom and mine. She stammers, her face sleepy and bewildered, as if she wasn't expecting to find me there and I'd pulled her from something private.

A stroll as the sun sets. Then, an outdoor movie. Her suggestion.

We set off walking together. She barely speaks.

I don't really know how to share so much intimacy with a body that shows no signs of wanting to be closer. This tension could dissolve if either of us walked away. Perhaps it should be me. I'm the only one who's not at home.

◆ ◆ ◆ ◆

I try asking her questions. The silence after the day's distance makes me nervous:

"Is there something you'd like? Something you don't have and you wish you did?"

"To live with a mare again. If the garden were big enough for her to be happy . . . I'd have to be sure I won't be traveling so much. The dog can come with me sometimes, if I go by car. She can do train trips, too, if they're not too long. Traveling with a mare is more complicated."

"Because horses travel by foot . . ."

"Yes, or in those trailers . . . Some are stable, those are fine. Others are total crap. Unstable, narrow. Imagine how it must be for them inside there, with the noise, the heat, and the movement. They are very sensitive animals; they grow resistant through violence, when they have no choice but to adapt, through repetition. They don't all adapt, of course. Some die. That is the human 'love' offered to animals: Adapt to my law or die."

". . ."

"The law of just one criterion and one possible language: ours. Or theirs, I should say. I am no longer really on the side of humans."

"I met an artist who painted silhouettes of horses with wings in black ink on recycled paper. She said the horses were angels."

"Was she beautiful?"

"Who? The artist?"

"Yeah."

"I imagine. Her idea is correct. She really hit the mark. That vigorous and fragile intelligence. Innocent, too, as if between two worlds . . . horses and angels. Horses must always be looked on with astonishment, like a vision. What kind of idiot would keep angels in stables?"

A childhood memory comes back to me. Horse-drawn carts waiting for tourists in southern Spain. The sight of heavy men who led them with long whips. A bag under their tails that held their feces during the ride.

"We'd gone to Córdoba for the Courtyards Festival—my father, my mother, my older brother, and me. I must've been six years old. It was the first time I'd been on a horse-drawn cart, and I was so excited. My father chose a very ornate cart pulled by a single white horse. Its driver was someone with a big belly beneath a tight shirt. All four of us got in. During the ride, I noticed the horse's panting and the sweat on its hindquarters. Its exertion. Suddenly, I realized: We were five bodies and a cart drawn by one single body. I burst into tears. I wanted to get down, but my parents encouraged me to keep going to the end of the route at the Alcázar de los Reyes Cristianos. But I couldn't bear it."

"And what did you do?"

"I pretended to be nauseous. I forced my throat into a position that looked like a convulsion. Finally I managed to actually provoke heaves and ended up vomiting on the leather seats. The driver stopped immediately, shouting. The puke was red- and orange-tinged. I'd had a lot of salmorejo at lunch."

"You like salmorejo? You were a wonderful little girl."

The satisfaction in her face as I told her the story. Her shining eyes and wide smile. Our conversation is strange, fragmentary and suspended. Filled with images. The closest thing to a conversation like this are the moments after two or three glasses of wine, alone with someone you'll kiss for the first time.

Her honey eyes, bulging beneath their lids, are more out of her face than in it. Her straight nose, thin-lipped mouth. I think there is something in that face that predisposes her to a type of convoluted pleasure, hard to access and very intense.

Pleasure and Time. Like the narrator in her book, the access would be difficult, the surrender contradictory, and the passion so strong that it leaves her broken.

Perhaps what I can give her would leave her exhausted, not broken.

And one can recover from exhaustion fairly easily. It's an acceptable risk.

We climb up to the castle, making time before the movie starts. She points to a ceramic sign with a dramatic gesture, exaggerating solemnity. She reads out loud in Catalan, in the voice messengers use in films when they read to kings, after having traveled a long, long way . . .

"'Altafulla: a small but pretty town on the Costa Daurada. With Roman and medieval traces. Good people, sensibility, and cultural inclinations.' What are you and I going to do with all these *cultural inclinations*, Photographer Girl? Tell me."

◆ ◆ ◆ ◆

We watch *El agua* on a projection screen set up in the church square. Before the movie starts some people greet her and she introduces me, articulating my name. I feel pleasure when I hear it spoken in her voice. A pleasure upon discovering something eventful, almost unprecedented: my name and her voice together. That it is possible. Also my elbow and hers, as we sit beside each other in two folding wooden chairs. Night has fully fallen, and we are together looking toward a screen, with her neighbors flanking us—the one with the tailor shop and the one with the English school for kids. As soon as the credits start to roll, they begin commenting on the movie, speaking to each other, their voices passing over us.

Then "Goodbye, goodbye, this was lovely"; "They could make a movie like that around here"; "Bye, bye."

She takes part in the conversation, but at the same time seems timid. Her voice sounds much quieter than the neighbors'. You can hardly hear the beginning of each sentence. A rustling of papers that begins to take shape as the other women fall silent and lean in slightly to hear better.

When we are alone, she leads me toward a restaurant's door. I head inside, thinking it's the place she's chosen for our dinner.

"They'll take good care of you here," she says. "I have to go."

Her freedom, her calmness, like a blow to the forehead. It is horrible to feel this way.

This is the contemporary author who's best captured the reality of passion? She's written all those scenes that bodies of various generations masturbate to. That's the woman I live with and who now prefers to spend hours lying on the sofa cuddling her dog over sleeping with me. Who shares almost nothing about her past, as if she had nothing to tell or as if she was returning traumatized from a conflict, having erased all the names.

I dine alone, make a lot of noise as I go back into the house, slamming the big blue door. I say nothing to the dog. I go to sleep without brushing my teeth.

We don't choose the first images that capture our desire.

They are imposed upon us: by happenstance, by power, or by norm.

I want to enter her very hard, not to momentarily flaunt a power I don't actually have, but to show my usefulness, my relevance here and now, the promise that I will be able to make her feel what she can't yet even imagine. Give the unique combination of our bodies the opportunity to produce new things. Things still impossible to predict.

Without her there to contradict me or be my co-conspirator, I imagine. And I imagine her the way I want to—wet lace beneath my fingertips as they travel along the embroidered shapes of the thread. I choose to imagine her wet because it's explicit. I can represent it with words; it seems to indicate a desire, hers for me.

I want to enter her hard, stay inside her for many hours,

almost relentlessly. To do that you must avoid the friction that ends up creating a burn on the flesh. How are we going to do it? Enduring, that the material endures as much as the fantasy demands. We fantasize with bodies that don't tire and split even in separate sleep, arms whose muscles don't flag, sexes sensitive enough to shudder and strong enough to not twinge or get harmed.

I imagine her body held up by her palms and knees on the soft surface of the bed. The ancient empire, the history of men never imagined a body like mine positioned behind one like hers, with my left hand holding her left hip and my right stroking her through her panties.

Insistent strokes, until she can't take it anymore and pushes back, seeking me out.

A hand loses its firmness only when it wants to. It can get tired, sure, but if she asks for more, I know I'll forget the tiredness and the pain. This trait defines my desire: I can disappear into her. Very attentive to all her expressions. Her sounds.

So focused, fucking her, I almost don't exist. I stop existing until the moment when, still on all fours, she turns her face back and looks at me. In that gaze, both hard and defeated by pleasure, she returns something to me, something like an identity, the feeling of possessing a life beyond what her name and body require of me.

"Give it to me carefully now. Give it to me slow."

The expression in her eyes, curious and slightly tired. She wants to feel it all, which is why she mentions *slow*ness.

I obey.

After a while, my left hand lowers from her hip to the hard flesh between her legs. My hand knows. It begins a hazy, circular caress while my right pushes and her thighs bounce back a little bit. I insist, stroking in circles, together riding the fire wave to keep it going.

Then the first whiplash.

She explodes between my fingers: I was asking for it, I'll admit.

Now I come thinking about the moment . . . a detail that, like the whole scene, I've invented: As the writer orgasms, her knees buckle, and she falls.

She drops onto the mattress and my arm is flattened beneath her belly.

I picture that very specific image to make myself come.

What does that say about me? What do the images that undo us say about us?

I dream of having my mouth filled; it is sweetness.

Three in the morning. I wake up uncomfortable but not nervous. Probably too hot, since I'm wrapped in a sheet that is now glued to me. A lick of nocturnal light slips through the shutters—waxing moon, bouncing against the garden, passing through the slit, and reaching the room's door, which I left slightly ajar.

Resting on the floor is the head of the dog, who moistens her snout with her tongue. She's seen me open my eyes. We scrutinize each other. Then she gets up and leaves.

I turn to one side, then the other, searching for a position I fail to find. An hour passes. Two. I pick up my phone, check my email, then Instagram. I answer a message from some girl I don't know. She says she likes my portraits in interior rooms. I think about it.

Then I stop thinking. *I'm on the coast, near Torredembarra, if you feel like coming here one of these days, I could take a few photos of you.*

I'm looking beyond. To maintain my health. I look beyond because perhaps a desire that will not materialize is already stealing my ability to see beyond the tunnel that frames the writer, her house, her world.

It is my third night here. I am aware of the velocity, of my impatience. I could leave tomorrow, filled with rage, give it all up as lost.

But who is capable of being patient? Patient as an exercise, patient when you grow impatient. I could expectantly await the progress toward the moment of doing actual things with her, but I cannot continue wondering if she really wants me here.

3.

A text message from her used to give me more pleasure than this uncomfortable corporeal reality. It was closer than this closeness. When the other writes to us, we imagine someone able to articulate those same things when speaking to us in close proximity, with an audible voice and the skin on their knee attentive to our hand.

In order to better understand why I am here, I need to go back in time, open up my email, read the messages over and over, peruse every detail with scientific thoroughness. I want to rescue some lost connotation, find a key, a clue:

August 3

I think you know something about images that I don't.
You have a brutal way of relating to them. How can
you take portraits of all those young girls for work,
at the service of brands, and not have a violent gaze?
Perhaps that small, arrogant place of shooting, through

a small window, is some sort of temptation that you can sometimes resist . . . and other times not. Where do you set the limits? Has any other woman ever given herself to you because you reflected back an image of her that she was unable to resist? And the opposite—have you failed to portray someone's beauty the way your naked eyes perceived it?

I'd like to know more. In your previous email, you said you work in digital, but you shoot your private images with film. Why is that?

I ask you these questions pretty much assuming you won't take as long with your reply as I'd like you to. You almost never answer with more than a simple sentence when I suggest murky things that could be discussed at great length . . . Perhaps I'm too probing, but I'll have patience with you.

It is so hot, I swear, my dog is lethargic and I'm dragging. I haven't done the shopping and a Sunday with just a package of almonds, a jar of broth, and the pantry empty is looming.

One day, someone I'm searching for also chooses me to sustain the intimacy of a conversation that becomes routine, although it occupies the edges of the day, morning, night. Our distanced communication accompanies the actions that *are* taking place; the supermarket, work, getting together with friends. She is constantly present, but as a ghost.

Her voice is the text poured into a chat on Instagram, that arrives in my WhatsApp, and when it deepens and invokes desire, it ends up password-protected from an outer gaze. Once her voice has known and occupied all those mediums, she begins to compose long emails. Emails that do not yet promise anything, but describe situations:

> *This morning I thought that it would be so lovely to be having breakfast together . . . The mail came and in it was the book on photography by Hervé Guibert you recommended, a blue object that now rests on the dining room table and suddenly seems to be the center of the house. Like you, before your visit.*

The promise is confined within the details that point at emotions. In the gestures of attention, of preference.

The abundance of our exchange of words means that the others, with whom we actually share our day-to-day, will no longer receive as much information. How can you tell someone else what is happening in a parallel reality where everything is chronicled, but in a more salacious tone than conventional conversations? We progressively trim the discourse we would typically share with the other women while an inner voice expands, increasingly taking center stage. Very soon, she gives me a certainty: There is always another message coming.

A writer who spends her time writing emails to a young woman she's never seen. I am that young woman. Now, here, this isn't the treatment I was expecting. Her body with no particular emotion, no frenzy. Wasn't I meant to receive another sort of attention? Wasn't I meant to be the favorite?

Because her language overwhelms, I imagined a body capable of surrender. I thought that, once I was here, she would lavish me with the same appreciation her words had offered.

Perhaps in person she didn't like me; perhaps she found me much less interesting. She can't locate the charm she saw in my photos. I know how to photograph myself, an advantage that, in the longer term, could turn out to be a liability.

She tells me that she's hosting a dinner party tonight for just a few friends. Some of them are coming from the city and have reserved several rooms at the Hotel Yola, by the beach. They want to spend the night instead of driving back.

She comes home from the market loaded down. In the kitchen, I help her unpack the full baskets. I already know where to put the oatmeal, the eggs, the fruit. I can complement her movements—that makes me feel good.

We boil chickpeas in a pressure cooker and prepare a big vegetable couscous. The room fills with the scent of cooked carrot—a scent I find quite unpleasant and she doesn't like either, so she turns on the extractor fan, opens the doors and windows.

"How lovely visits are, huh? But all this cooking is stressing me out. And it's not like I'm trying to impress anyone."

We wash tomatoes, chop basil.

"Like roommates." A chin lifts and falls, with some excitement. "I missed living with someone. Freely, each of us doing our own thing. From my experience, it's best that way."

I'm surprised that she could think there's anything in this house that could be described as "my thing" to place beside "her thing."

Any reason for existing that isn't driven by my desire for her.

The phone rings, announcing her arrival in ten minutes. In my stomach, unease and anticipation to discover the new features behind that name, something I've been desperately needing for some time. It is urgent I evaluate what that face holds, why that word is everywhere, as if there were only one person with a proper name in the writer's life. Did she ever mention her mother's, her grandmother's? *Greta, Greta, Greta.*

Greta is a body covered in clothes of many colors. A short pink-and-orange T-shirt. Pale blue jeans. Whatever her age, she is one of those people whose bodies are like a teenager's. Black syrup eyes and shoulder-length hair with bangs. A dark round mole on her chin. A formidable smile with large, crowded teeth. Because I'm drawn to her, because her image captivates me, I think the writer must be drawn to her as well.

She has a weightlessness to her, as if she finds life easy.

Two women with rounded eyeglasses and short hair walk through the rooms, checking out the walls.

"There are new things," they say. "Objects we've never

seen before, that weren't in the house when you lived here together."

Together? Who are they referring to?

"There was another house before this one," says Greta softly. "A serious and somewhat inaccessible house, a couple's home. She was in a long relationship before moving here and devoting herself to taking us all in all the time. Technically, she had more free time when she just had one girlfriend to look after, right?"

"I didn't bring many things from there. My mother's mirrors and a desk. I didn't need anything; I already had my drama and a puppy." She says that to the dog, whose eyes round off like marbles as she listens to the writer. When she finishes her sentence, she looks at me. "I didn't explain that part to you: I swapped a fifteen-year relationship for a house with paper-thin windows and a mutt. Two realities with which she would never have wanted to coexist."

She says she already wrote about that story in the novel I read. That once you go over and over something upsetting and draining enough times, you start to lose interest. That boredom is a fundamental part of the therapeutic process. That "enough" times are many, many times, and very draining. And, as her grandmother used to always say, "patience is the companion of wisdom." That it is a simple truth.

But the part about the separation wasn't what interested me about her novel; in fact, I barely remember it. I was drawn in later, by affinity and at the same time by distance. The mother who dies and her absent daughter, who is unable to be with her because she is too afraid to face reality. A young student with strong hands, whom the woman meets up with by night, in the recently acquired house. The ardor in the narrator's voice as she feels herself absolutely guilty and in surrender to the sexual. All the demands of a capricious child met in the place where the mother offered only a void. Their obsession with fusing, pursued through every gate their bodies offer.

I wasn't a young man, in the traditional sense of the term.

I saw two paths of identification with the text; on one hand, I could be that young man; my talent and my needs coincided with his.

My mother had also passed away a year ago, of the same illness. Unlike the narrator, I had been by her side, right up until the final moment. Although initially I, too, had feared the image, I'd stayed until the very end. I had seen it all.

The temperature has dropped and some thunder marks the start of a storm. Is it still a summer storm? The writer opens a bottle of bourbon and places a couple of dark chocolate bars on the table.

"Here's dessert, my dears. No one remembered to bring any, so we'll have to have it my way."

Greta is a scriptwriter, jovial, open. She effortlessly receives the attention of the writer and the four other guests. For a long time my gaze is hers. I follow her movements with concern, with interest. She tells me she has been writing a series with several seasons.

"Many intellectuals aren't at all impressed by any of this, because they consider it a *lesser* form of writing. But our friend is; she can see the value of enchantment in everything."

She points to our host, and our host addresses me to give me context. It seems she feels responsible for ensuring I have the same information as the rest of the group:

"She's in the middle of a difficult project. A series for young people with a lot of sex scenes and experimentation in violent contexts. Greta was the first screenwriter to ask to work with an intimacy coordinator. The coordinator is not only mediating and protecting the actresses and actors on set, but she also, in this case, writes the intimate scenes with her. Isn't that fascinating? I wish I could have a coordinator working with me on the sex scenes in my novels, too. To make sure everyone is okay and no one gets hurt—not the characters, not me, not my future readers . . ."

"Ha, ha, don't be so silly . . ."

"No, seriously, Greta, listen, it makes sense. Maybe it could help me avoid getting canceled."

"They aren't going to cancel you, babe. Your writing is opaque, and if no one can understand it, no one can be offended by it. We live in the era of Pornhub. One video a day before bedtime. Then sleep tight."

"My books have been criticized for having too many sex scenes."

"Don't worry about that, there can never be too many if a lesbian's writing them. We have a deficit of content to begin with. But I'll put you in touch with the coordinator. She is precise and empathetic. And she commits to her work . . . She will help you see things that you wouldn't otherwise . . ."

At some point in the evening, the conversation begins to exhaust me. Everyone is speaking loudly, and they have a lot to say to each other. I'm starting to feel sleepy. They change the music and put on Ángeles Toledano, the singer-songwriter's voice winding its way as she softly sings a bambera. Greta says she's met her. That she once had dinner with her in Madrid. That gets the guests excited; they want to know more, and she answers dramatically, with an air of mystery. One song leads to the next, with lyrics about holding tightly to the roots hidden beneath the earth—not the branches, because the wind takes those away.

"Well, you, my friends, were the branches, and you sank into the earth with me."

"All the same: branch and root, root and branch."

"Toward the sun and toward the depths."

As they sing and talk and show how much they adore each other, how together they form part of something bigger, I stand up like someone completely anonymous and slip into one corner of the room, where the dog is dozing. I gradually slide next to her, and she moves her ears slightly, not lifting her snout from the floor. We are two shapes of similar length.

I lightly rub her head. The messy little hairs on the top. Then I stroke her gently between the eyes. She lets me touch her for the first time.

◆ ◆ ◆ ◆

The writer holds a glass of bourbon in one hand and looks at us gently from above. It is a kind of gaze that makes her seem to occupy a bubble of exception; she is completely surrounded by a slower kind of time.

"You are both going to fall asleep here. Come on, I'll take you up to your room."

We walk, shoulder very close to shoulder, through the hallway. Then we hear the window in my room bang, and it takes me a few fractions of a second to remember that I left it wide open, that it's been storming hard for a while now, and that the bed is perfectly exposed to the rain.

There are two echoes of words. Two melodies sounding at the same time. One is the sentence spoken before arriving, all the hope in an offer: "Come on, I'll take you . . ." The other is a single expression, tossed out harshly as we cross through the arch of the door: "Shit." Both lines of phantasmagorical sound are spoken by the same voice; they are trapped in a mental cloud while I contemplate the scene, not knowing what to do.

The writer has closed the window and the shutter; she's pulled out a small hair dryer from a dresser drawer; she's unplugged the lamp on the bedside table and plugged in the hair dryer so she could run the hot air first over the pillows, then the sheets, the mattress cover, and finally the mattress.

I look toward the glass with a bit of alcohol and a squalid ice cube that's almost completely melted on the carpet while the dog sniffs it from a prudent distance. Still and useless, I then observe a woman dedicated to the tedious task of getting the dampness out of a bed where she probably isn't going to sleep, because lovers in their urgency leap into wet beds, or avoid the dampness and migrate to some other part of the house together, but they don't engage so kindly in serving the other as they would a guest.

A bowl of soup and a spoon. Warm sheets in the middle of a storm.

Everything has been handed to me, and yet . . .

I wake up with the sensation of having lost.

It is desire; I've experienced this before. It manifests as suspense in the abdomen.

It's similar to the void left by something that's lost, and also to the confusion over something that's failed.

It has to be from before. This pain has to be from before, since she has done nothing but take care of me. What can I do for her?

What she won't allow me to.

4.

"A dazzling morning," she said. Dazzling with its intense glare.

Greta will arrive in two hours, to take us to a concert and then to the mountains. Nobody has asked me. Everything has been decided for me.

The plan is to drive along the coastline to a small theater in a seaside town—a pianist will be playing there at nine. They've reserved a hotel for the first night. The next day: breakfast, a swim, and continuing on to Tavertet. We have to prepare light luggage, with clothes for three days. We'll spend the next night in the mountains, at a retreat center.

"A large, shared house, several cabins in a forest of holm oaks, and a meditation room with objects from Nepal. The community hasn't taken monastic vows—some of them studied philosophy in Barcelona and took a different path than expected.

They dared to commit to a collective life project. But we won't tell you any more. It's best you see it for yourself."

They bring two bags out of the writer's bedroom, made of hard thread, like fishing line. Bags with colorful strips and a rigid handle that still seems flimsy. While she and Greta fill one on the dining room table, they give me the empty one.

"If you have room, we'll put the dog's blanket and things in there; don't worry if not. They won't give off an odor; her food will go somewhere else."

The dog and me. Sitting in the back seat. She lowers her head and rests one of her paws on my knee. It is a soft, heavy paw. We are the daughters.

On the way, there was only one hotel on the coast that allows dogs and had a vacancy for the night. It turned out to be a place the writer appreciates, run by women for generations. A hotel where the clients are usually regulars, stay for several days, eat a special dish of fries served with a pot of mussels, and read on the terrace alongside animals varying in size. This is the description we get of the place, which Greta already knows: "She always reserves the hotel," she says. "I wouldn't dare deprive her of that pleasure. I'm in charge of the daytime, and the nights are all hers."

I'm sure I can hear pride in that "nights are all hers." Sticky words that get caught in the channel of the spoken. She plays with language, her features provocative: her little rounded nose, her lips supple and focused on the center of her mouth; the corners, however, fade into her face. She wears white-framed sunglasses with the logo of a flashy brand on one earpiece. A tight spaghetti-strap shirt marks the abundant curve of her chest. From the back seat I wonder what I would've thought of her if I'd seen her for the first time in a different context, outside of the house, without being secretly irritated.

I'm jealous of something I can easily make out under her clothes, a turgidity in her thighs resting on either side of the steering wheel. That firmness, I learned as a teenager but confirmed in a more brutal way in my thirties, gives an advantage. An unnamable advantage, undesirable for those of us who want to flee the gender system, forget . . . Is she important to the writer? What is it that she likes?

We arrive at the hotel and check in with very little time to spare; we still have a decent walk to the square where the theater is. In the family suite, I observe my fate: a room with two spaces united by an open door. The double bed and the kids' room on the other side.

"It's not an extra bed, like in other places. It's a triple room for three adults," the writer informs me, excusing herself. It seems she is trying to interrupt my inner voice as it interprets the space. She has brought us here and now divvies us up in this way. The two of them sharing intimacy and me a few feet away.

It is a simple place, a classic coastal summer design in blues and whites, with no decoration that breaks the line of the vintage wardrobes, with the scent of the sea.

◆ ◆ ◆ ◆

Convincing the dog to stay in the room alone takes twenty minutes of petting and a long gristle of dry ox skin that she doesn't even touch. The writer asks at the reception desk for someone to keep an eye on her; she does so with an elegant expression and a very even-tempered voice, so the receptionist herself offers to walk the dog around dinnertime, at the end of her shift.

"Thank you so much. That's so kind. What a shame, but I can't accept. She won't go for a walk with you if she doesn't know you. All she'd do is bark, make a scene, and bother the other guests. She doesn't have that type of innocent, friendly personality all dogs supposedly have."

She dictates her cell phone number so they can keep her updated. As she does, I try to see if I can memorize it.

I'm hungry. We barely ate on the road—they had some walnuts and a box of figs in the car—and we rushed out of the shared family suite. I search the depths of my backpack for a blue Sugus that I grabbed from a jar at the reception desk. I feel around amid a ton of particles and little bits of trash until I happen upon its square shape and bring it to my mouth with excitement.

We are going on empty stomachs because they're unwilling to be late to the concert, to make noise coming in, to mix that noise with the music that comes out of the piano. I don't really care. I experience my curiosity from a distance, feeling like a nobody, someone transparent whom others can't perceive and who can't shift the course of events, no matter what she does. There is something comfortable in this stance if it weren't for the hunger that accompanies it. I let myself be led; I barely take part in the conversations. My shyness turns me into a voyeur. Near the entrance to the theater, I go up to a small kiosk and ask for a chocolate bar. I feel the sugar flowing. I decide to relax. I remain silent. I don't even go to my phone to find the concert tickets in a shared WhatsApp chat; I trust they will do that for me. I get lazy. I hope that they'll want to drink wine tonight at dinner.

She wears her hair short below her ears and pulls part of it back into a tiny bun. Her clothes are elegant and neutral, pants and a vest, all black, even her loafers. It is her mannish shoes I focus my gaze on, how they move as she pushes the pedal.

The pianist follows the standards of a classical recital, but alternates the *Oiseaux tristes* by Ravel with *Études* 5 and 6 by Glass. I don't know any of those pieces. I compulsively look at the program I picked up at the entrance, knowing I might need it for a future conversation.

I see the writer's profile, her brow furrowed in concentration and her lips parted. She often tilts her head slightly as if that would allow her to get a better look at the hands playing, but we are in a blind spot, and the whole hand only appears when raised during the pause that follows an arpeggio. I look toward the pianist's loafer and think that I'd like to meet her, that we could be friends. I also wonder if she is the type of person who could end up being the writer's lover. I think she could.

I feel an electric shock in my sex and then the heat of rage in my temple.

As it ends, three rounds of applause. Amid the celebrations of the audience, the writer curves toward us to whisper, "The encore will be a piano version of *Lamento della Ninfa*. Let's imagine the nymph is one of us. Her lament repeats because somewhere she holds on to the hope that her pain will lessen or that there is someone capable of responding to her call. There is no lament without the hope of someone hearing it. The complaint and the longing are constructed musically thanks to an ostinato that pervades everything. The ostinato is a stubborn repetition of four descending notes. This is how the lament takes shape: la-sol-fa-mi. In the first repetition the hope falls on the third note, insistent, returning. 'Love, love, she cries to the heavens. And thus, in the heart of the lovers, love mixes fire and ice.' That is what the end of the sung portion says. Fire-ice eros, sweet-bitter eros. On the piano the interpretation is more abstract."

Her prediction comes true. The pianist sits down before the instrument and waits a few moments while gazing out into the void, then begins to move her fingers. The ostinato of her left hand repeats throughout the piece, persevering, sustaining the posture while the right hand dances.

✦ ✦ ✦ ✦

"She must be a lesbian." Those are Greta's first words as we exit. "She has that eccentric, deviant virtuosity. She plays by heart and in her own way."

"I think she's sad," answers the writer. "She's suffered, but she retains her passion; her choice of program speaks of truncation and fantasy."

Suddenly I find it odious, her way of speaking about a stranger as if she had some unusual access into the pianist's life. The writer, someone who knows and has experience, who is above good and evil. What she says must be false. Oracular posturing that makes her always seem in control of reality. She thinks she can read others' minds. But no, she can't control what's real; only her telling of it.

I feel guilty for thinking these things. Where does this rage come from? Does the conversation justify it, or the tone? Or do I just feel excluded? Forced to look beyond, while she and I barely look at each other. There isn't time for us to look at each other amid so many other people.

And how would it be if it were different? I try to imagine. If through Greta's body, which partitions us like a wall, the writer were to hold my gaze for a few complicit seconds. It would be like something on the tongue melting triumphantly. The chosen ones, who move confidently because they do not doubt the reciprocity of desire. Two who look at each other and hold each other's gaze because they know that sooner or later they will be alone together, poured out onto each other.

And because they know that, they enjoy the interruption. All that time with a third or fourth person who seeks attention. Showing patience, feigning interest toward something beyond the wait, blinded by each other.

But that's not us, not yet.

Who are we?

It's already night and the rest of the concertgoers have left the theater. We wait for a little while at the exit, in the middle of the street, the three of us in a line, three pieces in a board game.

Greta speaks ironically, raising her voice. "I know how you are—your historical preference for languid virtue, passion, and anemia. Such tastes hint at a perverse personality, my little friend, and they're obsolete."

Little of her verbiage makes sense, even though I understand everything she's saying. It's arrogant, sectarian humor—their humor and not mine—that exposes the obscenity of my being outside, of being a guest.

We could have been kindred spirits, but the pianist will write to whom I don't want her to, and the pianist will join our dinner. Consistent with the logic up until now, the plan will be announced to me without asking, assuming that it is good news for all of us. Dining together, oh yes, dreamy. Who wouldn't want to dine with an elegant and somewhat sad pianist? I will pray for someone to stop her on the way from the theater to the outside table where we are seated. That she will never arrive.

What I pray for doesn't come to pass.

Later she will be before us. And she will be timid and gentle but perceptive and amusing every time she speaks. I will constantly examine her, unable to control myself, unable to stop myself. I search for signs that would make her exceptional—in other words, more attractive than me. I focus on her eyes, which must be clear in the sunlight, even though their color is indistinguishable in the terrace at night. If we see her again tomorrow, if the evening continues and she comes with us to the bedroom, at breakfast those almost yellow eyes will be a sparkling blue that will ruin everything.

I wonder what brought her to this table. What sort of interest keeps her attentive hours after a concert. They order salad and a large platter of croquettes. I beeline toward the food. The outside crunches and the inside is a lava of bechamel with mushrooms, with cheese and spinach, or with squid ink.

While they talk, I eat. At first nimbly and with conviction, firmly digging into the platter, knowing that I am taking my share. Later I lose count because they've all stopped eating even though half of the croquettes are still on the plate. It's a generous serving, where my pilfering could go on unnoticed. The pianist is no longer eating and the writer seems to be nourished simply by her gaze. I think that both of them are beyond the world where I, very alone, breathe and live. I contemplate them sidelong until I can barely hear the pianist's voice, which moves into the background, my attention focused on the last three croquettes.

They all end up in my mouth, one by one, without asking, without guilt.

And I could have eaten many more. I simply eat all the ones that are on the platter: That is the measure of my hunger. All the ones that are there and the phantasm of a couple more that would truly sate me.

I remember myself as a girl on the beach. My mother had put a red Mickey Mouse visor on me and hung a small plastic container around my neck with a string. The container was filled with peanuts. It was part of my lunch, or all of it, I don't know. To my disgust, Mamá tried to convince me that the serving of nuts was all I needed nutritionally. My response to her restrictions was usually ambiguous. Wasn't she always acting in my best interests? The frustration of my hunger made me want to cry. On the other hand, I was proud that we both ate the same thing. I was a handful of peanuts closer to turning into her, a slender and flirtatious being. When the mothers of my friends would pull out containers of homemade breaded chicken and potato omelets to share with their daughters on the beach, mine would open up a bag of nuts and some cans of beer. After the second can, her mood would start to change. She would become irascible. She would get angry because I let sand get into my backpack or because I had forgotten to rinse my swimsuit in the shower before putting it away. Looking at me with displeasure, Mamá would say I was a disaster.

Disaster. My chubby legs and feet beside my mother's body. My backpack filled with sand and the remains of a snack from the day before, gum wrappers. I was off in the clouds and wasn't present at what was being celebrated. My gaze beneath the Mickey Mouse visor was always aimed somewhere else, at the girls eating chicken fillet, potato salad, and lemon cake on a foldable table brought from home, with their parasol, their lounge chairs, and their cooler.

With the beer and cigarette in her hands, her sunglasses and long curly hair with its gleaming red highlights, she looked like a movie star. I equally admired my mother's sculpted abdomen and the other girls' breaded chicken fillets. If I had to choose between the two, I wouldn't be able to make up my mind. What did seem to be true is that my body was more made for eating than for being lovely in that way.

"Keep your eyes on yourself," my mother would say, adjusting my jelly sandals. "Don't envy those girls. If they're learning to eat with no limitations now, wait until they're grown up; they'll be as bad as their mothers. It's easy to be as skinny as a rail when you're little, but in a few years, they'll have lost that. You have to have willpower and good genes. You're lucky to have the latter, but don't ruin yourself. You have to learn how to eat what you need. No more and no less."

I didn't see anything wrong in those other women; their abundance, their joy in eating and sharing, seemed normal. Secretly, I thought that if there was anything strange in that landscape, it must be us, always so alone, not talking to anyone, two towels on the sand and a can of Mahou beer for an ashtray. Yes, how strange and exclusive, somewhat arrogant, my mother's presence beneath the sun, and mine, her awkward cherub squire. How to satisfy my mother? Shaking out the towel well before putting it into the bag, restraining my desires, appearing grateful, admitting to a certain moral superiority in her way of seeing the world.

It is true that I did it with certain pleasure, paying her my respects, if in exchange she rewarded me with her cuddles. To win her favor, I complied with her law and was proud to do so. When she was around, I fasted, and then at my grandmother's house—without having to ask permission, since it was set out for me—I would open up the pantry where she kept the black baking chocolate, the tins with anise pastries, the packages of cupcakes and meringue desserts, the cream cookies, and the bags of ghost-shaped Cheetos.

On my knees in front of the pantry, with the urgency of someone who fears she'll be interrupted, I would eat, eat, eat.

Greta yawns, they stand up, we say goodbye to the pianist, and the three of us return to the hotel together. When we get there, they are so tired there's no time for tensions, not even for the strangeness of a first time sleeping together. The room is large and my single bed is close enough to theirs that I can hear them breathing. We brush our teeth, the two of them in the bathroom and me in the middle of the room. We take turns rinsing. They hug me good night and then each of us changes into our pajamas without looking at the others.

That's it. Pretty easy in the end. I'm not sure what terrible thing I was expecting. I'm trapped in the waiting for something wonderful or something terrible. I feel ridiculous but calm. I will sleep well tonight.

5.

We travel along a winding road. Greta falls silent with the steering wheel in her hands, trying to focus. When she drives, she seems older, responsible for everyone, while the rest of us regress to childhood. The writer is the navigator and fiddles with Google Maps and reads directions out loud, often with an imprecision that wavers between unbearable and amusing. Greta scolds her a little, very firmly saying, "Please, make an effort to understand the directions. Otherwise just put it here in front of me and I'll look at them myself."

I sit in the back, hopelessly trying to hide my nausea from the others. The truth is I have a headache and my mouth is starting to salivate with increasing insistence. If we don't stop now, soon will come the reflux, then the heaves, finally the vomit.

I announce my situation in a weak voice that clearly conveys how borderline it is. I keep my lips nearly closed as I speak, fearing that if I open my mouth any more, I'll lose control. They quickly stop in a rural area, not waiting to reach a town. Being able to activate the handle and lunge through the open door seems almost a miracle, one that arrives right at the limit of a change in state.

When my feet hit the ground, I suddenly start to retch. I feel exposed by what my stomach brings up, so, without much time to think, I swallow. I swallow like a liar or a thief, because I can't bear to be someone who empties herself out in front of them. They don't love me. You can't vomit in front of someone who doesn't love you enough to be by your side without repulsion. At the same time, in my memory of holding back my drunk friends' hair in dirty bar bathrooms, the truth is I didn't feel repulsion. I felt it was a privilege to be the only one with access to such excessive intimacy: I was the one chosen to go with them to vomit.

I was never able to flip the scene and occupy the other role. When I was feeling ill, before it was too late, I would quickly flee the bar, writhing, to some alley where I could empty my stomach in a dark doorway, alone. Then I would return and try to reincorporate myself into the night as if nothing had happened.

They aren't monks; they aren't celibate; they only wear robes during ceremonies. There is a meditation at eight in the morning and another at eight in the evening. They have a vow of silence between waking and the start of breakfast. If I see someone during those hours, I shouldn't be surprised if they don't say good morning.

The writer speaks with a lot of emotion. It's obvious she is extremely fond of the community. We are about to arrive.

◆ ◆ ◆ ◆

We are welcomed by a young woman with a soft voice, who walks toward us slowly. Then we're greeted by the countryside surrounding a stone house and an enormous set table by its entrance. The tablecloths are blue and yellow. There are wildflowers in small jars and, on a side table, several trays of grilled vegetables, vegetarian protein, and mashed potatoes with maitakes.

Another young, svelte brunette, with a long braid and an apron, sings out the ingredients as she looks us in the eye. Hers is a friendly gaze, without any particular intent. I'm always surprised by those gazes that don't seem to want anything from others. I choose a random seat among the people and feel my blood pressure drop, some sort of a break. We've gone from that tense solitude of three to being able to be part of something. I'm reminded of my shared apartment on Paral·lel. Five folx living together. That calm familiarity that I definitely miss.

An old mastiff approaches, and the writer's dog, who was resting in the sun, sits up wagging her tail in greeting. She sniffs beneath her ear carefully.

Several people stand up for seconds. They return with their plates full. "We eat a lot here. One of the best things is the food."

My hunger doesn't stand out. I serve myself some more mashed potatoes.

The young woman with the sweet voice asks the writer a question. Something happened with a post on social media that's getting negative comments. She asks me, "What do you think?" But I don't know.

She says, "While they focus on hating, we'll focus on loving and working, which are the same thing. To keep loving while they try to destroy your name, you have to turn, look toward the world, but the world of things, not of opinions. Look at the hardwood table, the water that comes tepid out of the tap—all those things remain unaltered while the comments on an Instagram profile change."

It must be the countryside and the company. I feel good.

She pointed to me as she said it: "The two of us are staying." What was she answering? What was the question? Did I hear her correctly? Yes, I could hear the woman with the soft voice asking her, "Do you want to stay in the cabin where you did the retreat? *Your* cabin." They both laughed. Her teeth, so pretty. In her smile, the upper lip gathered, the lower one full. I wish I could give her that satisfaction, too. She addresses me: "Does that sound good to you?"

"Yeah, and what about Greta?"

"She will sleep in the main house—she knows it well. She'll be fine."

"The space is small even for two, definitely not big enough for three," confirms the young woman with the soft voice. I look at the writer and then I look at Greta, who is chatting with a young man a few chairs down. Everything seems mysteriously tranquil. As if I were the only one pierced through by passion.

◆ ◆ ◆ ◆

Now we leave the lunch table, walk down a path beside a small gray mountain. Dusk is falling and the light is lovely and warm. We are entering the forest, little branches and small undergrowth crunch beneath our feet. As we walk, grasshoppers leap aside—there are two, three, that take flight with each step. When we arrive, someone sweeps the ground outside a small wooden construction above three stairs.

It is too small of a space for us to be alone inside without yet sharing the intimacy of lovers. A single room holds the gas stove, the table with two chairs, the heater, and the double bed. The bathroom is in another section. It occurs to me I could slip in there and take a very long shower. Meanwhile, she could decide what to do or who to be in that narrow space.

I let the water run for five, ten minutes more than I need to. I try to imagine what her expression will be when I come out of the bathroom wrapped in a towel. But when I do, she isn't there, trapped between four walls with me, but outside, lying in a hammock beneath a holm oak.

I get dressed. I go out with her. We exchange a few words every once in a while. The sun will set and, when night begins to be truly black, the woman with the long braid will come through the forest with a big basket filled with food.

There is hot pumpkin puree and escalivada with rice. She also brings breakfast for tomorrow: tomatoes from the garden, a bowl of hummus, apples, cereal, and nuts. A dark bread already sliced.

Who is this writer? Someone who seems calm, or who acts calmly to help us. Both of us, who are involved in this. A wanting to be together without knowing in what terms. I begin to understand something about what she offers: a presence with a promise.

But who is she? Someone who understands the awkwardness and suggests a rite of passage. Turning on the gas, making some herbal tea before sleeping. She invites me into the game with an instruction: "Look in those jars, they have plants gathered locally."

I choose thyme for its strong smell, dark color. My choice satisfies her. It's what she would have suggested.

At some point I must have fallen asleep. I can't remember, but I wake up suddenly with a strong urge to take a piss. There is a pressure in my abdomen. I feel restless and aroused after spending hours so close. We are in the dark, and I can't see her well, but I breathe in the smell of a rose oil she bought on a trip to Morocco. Her hair is, like mine, strewn over the pillow. We could tangle ourselves together and yet, we remain separated. Every strand of her hair, like every strand of mine, unknotted. I know because I walk alone; I can sit up, direct my movements toward the bathroom. Nothing ties me to her body, only my attention.

When I get back into bed, I am able to do it. I do it: I move closer to her back and fit myself to her as she rests on one shoulder, on her side. Her silent breathing makes me think she is awake. I decide to draw closer because something stubborn inside me demands it, and perhaps she desires it, too. First, the lower part of my stomach touches her back, and then I lift my folded legs to fit behind her thighs. It is a perceptible advance, although I try to do it delicately, not wanting to wake her, suspecting that she isn't sleeping.

The position offers a nice place, a simple place. Now that we aren't forced to speak, or look into each other's eyes, perhaps we can have this conversation, which is said in a different way.

But she does not move. Not even a small gesture of her body responds—in other words, her body does not speak. And if she is awake, and her silence is voluntary, then isn't her stillness a message?

It was a mistake. I'm invading her intimacy. What am I doing, curled up like a baby around an adult who does not offer tenderness in return? How heavy my arousal feels in this embrace that cannot be innocent and yet is: the pressure near the bladder, the dampness, the guilt.

I choose to wait. *Please, say something.* Giving up hope, I move one fingertip forward, not carelessly but as if I were truly confident we shared a space of intimacy. I advance from the abyss, moving only forward, because only forward lies the possibility of a definitive, radical response, be that what it may. The tip of my middle finger advances along the back of her hand. *Please, please, please.*

Meaning, fate, electrifies my finger. I am going to shock the opaque body of the other. Force it (to respond: either pull away or let me continue). I am going to force her body to enter into conversation, in the game of meaning: I am going to make it speak. Finally, fragments of a lover's discourse.

Let her shout a *no* that I never stop hearing. Let her be terrible, clear. Let her mark a distance with bite marks and blood.

She murmurs a little groan, like the one the sleeping dog makes when someone sits beside her on the sofa and moves her. Then she advances her hand and grabs my forearm. Stuck together like that, she stills again and sighs.

At some point, strangely oblivious to the exceptionality of the moment, I will also fall asleep.

Greta comes to help us carry some things: the remaining food, the garbage, the luggage.

She smiles and is kind despite having slept alone. She says she slept so, so well. That she dreamt of something falling from the sky, something that was spongy like a cake, and we all gathered it up. She says that she can't wait to live in community, like here, all of us together. That it has to happen long before old age, that we have to find a place, a space.

Her happiness makes me feel like a monster, a deviant version of the possessive beast inflamed by evil. Who wouldn't prefer Greta when she remains uncorrupted, like nothing could scare her or make her jealous, or vicious, or always think the worst the way I do?

It is not only a certain type of beauty. There is something more that I lack and that Greta could give her: a generous and light nature.

We head toward the others.

The writer is wearing shorts. I focus on a scratch on the back of her thigh, right above the knee. The other morning, while swimming in a river pool, she scraped against some rocks. The mark looks like a scratch from a big feline, the track of a claw or the clamp of a bramble that, like a carnivorous plant, was determined not to release its prey.

I walk behind her. I don't want to stop looking at her curved lines, a tiny trail of scabs. If our relationship were different, I could come up behind her and place my hand on her, feeling my way, half caressing, half starting something more. I could anxiously await nighttime, rest my soft mouth right there on the rock's bitemark. She could laugh.

From the mountain back to the beach. This hedonistic wandering must be normal for her lifestyle, her way of moving through the world. Having access to salad, to tuna ceviche. Beer, mussels, and a shared slice of cheesecake, after which we decided to take a dip. In my tendency to feel marginalized and undesirable, beer facilitates a predisposition to friendship. Perhaps the normal way they feel is how I do after drinking a beer on an empty stomach.

When the check comes, the writer doesn't let me pay my part. She says I didn't choose this plan or these expenses.

None of us has a swimsuit, but her situation is the most complicated—she's not wearing a bra and her panties, very high-cut on the ass, are white. Our underwear is dark: Greta is wearing two pieces and I've just got one.

The writer undresses in front of a group of men and women who are watching their grandkids and looking out at the horizon. In other words, she unbuttons her long shirt, lowers her pants, places the folded clothes on a rock, and I stare at my feet in the sand, so as to not scratch her with my eyes. Greta laughs. "A white thong, the most unsuitable for this context, but you're gorgeous, my love." The writer's wavy hair lies on her naked chest, which I glance at out of the corner of my eye for the first time—small, with nipples firm enough to peek out amid the golden highlights. She doesn't hesitate to get into the water.

Greta follows her; as a straggler, I have the chance to remain at the perfect distance to glimpse the white fabric that reflects the light, her narrow waist, her full thighs and round ass—the ass of a swimmer or dancer, not of someone who spends, who *must* spend many hours a day sitting and working. But I've already seen clearly that my writer and her gorgeous fifty years of flesh do not believe in chairs or sacrifice. At least not that sort of sacrifice.

◆ ◆ ◆ ◆

Each of us stays afloat in the sea in our own way. Each of us has a technique. Greta moves her arms in wide half circles; the writer seems to be kicking her feet and keeps the upper part of her body still. I stop floating and dive. I descend to move around.

From the water you can see a row of small little houses clinging to the beach—the homes of tiny people, of gnomes with hammocks in the sand, colorful houses that before too long will be snatched by the sea. Today we look at them.

A long shirt allows her to discreetly remove her wet thong in front of the grandparents. She's jumping up and down while she pulls up her pants without any underwear, swearing with a pitiful voice that the salt will cut her skin in the car, that her skin will end up irritated.

The writer opens the back door to sit with me. I will no longer travel alone with the dog. Greta will be a taxi driver, and I will no longer be a little girl driven to the beach by her mothers.

There is something different in her face, a relaxation that fixes a smile onto her gums, unchanging, constant, madcap, internal.

In the car, hot from the sun, she takes off her damp sandals and makes a surprised expression. She draws close to my face, pretends to cover my nose with her fingers, laughing. "Hold your breath, they stink really bad." I can't smell it, I tell her; that's the typical thing only you can smell on yourself, even though you worry others can. I don't tell her that I'm thinking about my sex, about the often-brazen scent of my sex, a scandal with no consequences or record.

Her hand moves from my nose to my hand. She rests its weight there briefly, running three fingers over its back. Middle, thumb, and index advance. I look at her longish fingernails, then at a braid of gold like a wedding ring.

Finally her hand chooses me. Is this really happening? What changed? Why now and why before, so many times before, did it take a detour?

The three of us continue talking about the trip, about the landscape. I try to maintain the conversation so that the intimacy of our hands won't fully take center stage, soon becoming too much, and have to stop. Which is why I tell her, "Look, look at the windows of that house, the blue and the yellow—look at the collapsed roof of that one. It's a shame all these old houses are left to rot; it's a shame." I tell her what she wants to hear. It's a prayer to keep her fingertips now fiddling on the membrane that links my pinky with the rest of my body. At the same time, my thumbnail brushes her palm, a thumb that is mine against what is hers, a thumb with its moment in the conversation, that enters to finally articulate without any shyness: *I am not a dead hand. I am not just a friendly hand. See the future's certainty in a lover's hand; I can show my willingness by remaining very still, sustaining the caress.*

"Look, a bird-sighting spot. A woman walking with a cane,

binoculars hanging around her neck." She maintains the touch, but I think the retreat is surely approaching. It must be time for her to get tired of it; we're already halfway there.

But the expected rejection never comes. She doesn't pull away; she is resting her head on my shoulder when it comes time to laugh. She brings her other hand over and, now, yes, she captures both of mine within hers.

While all this is happening, I observe her obliquely: It is not likely we can sustain a shared gaze while my index finger makes circles on one of her knuckles. It is not likely the caress will continue after the car, once the doors are open, when the driver releases the steering wheel. I am not going to look at her if later my mouth cannot calmly follow the direction of my eyes. I will no longer be able to connect without my mouth, without sucking her lips, bringing her fingers to the edge of my teeth.

Feigning a shared conversation is the only way to resolve this tension that's been created. How absurd it would be if it were to halt here.

Ahh, but thank you, thank you. I'm grateful for the tension, the vortex, like the crease made in a little girl's belly by a swing's upward trajectory as its unoiled chain squeaks.

"Look toward the edge of the road. Imagine that on the scattered dirt there is a mother boar and hundreds of voles—look, the light is still holding." Look there and here, but please, don't look at me directly when I speak to you. I don't know how to go on; how not to bring you to my mouth; how not to ask from the wet depths of my tongue, continue the conversation from there.

It seems that someone who is not her, and not me, holds the authority over this moment.

But who?

And what if I draw closer and do it? Kiss her. I haven't the faintest idea what would happen.

But it isn't that obvious; it isn't that easy. Reading the signs, terrified that it's all just a misunderstanding, a grotesque gap between my imagination and hers.

We're almost there. Will it be tonight?

The dog is glued to me; she no longer follows her. I go to the cabinet where the dog's food is kept and serve her some. It is a damp pouch filled with bits of steamed vegetables and turkey. I love the sound the moist food makes as it falls onto the plate. She gets very close, sniffs without touching the food before gorging. I watch her eat; it's comforting.

Greta stays for dinner. She said it's very difficult to part after such a lovely trip like the one we made. Now she rummages through the pantry as if it were hers, sticks her fingers into a jar of artichoke hearts in water, pulls one out, brings it to her mouth.

Then she opens the kitchen window. She smokes. She is messy and the writer tolerates her.

Go. Go. Go.

The sooner the better. Greta, go.

She serves herself a glass from the bottle of wine that was stored in the dish cabinet. It is the first time we drink alcohol at home on a regular day, and it took another person to make it happen.

Privacy is impossible. I get angry. I feign tiredness and go to my room. I wish she would leave. I hope she doesn't sleep over. Before I arrived to this house, she was sleeping in my place . . . Would they sleep together if she stays?

In the bedroom whose threshold I have yet to cross.

I hear both of their voices in a clumsy whisper heading to the room. They are laughing. I hate their laughter. I feel rage and also resentment on the edges of my skin.

I am aroused, but I decide not to touch myself. As revenge. I am going to renounce that sensation and the images it unleashes.

Ciao ciao, I'm out. I swear I'm done. With this weird story, with these people.

The night is dry in my eyes and acidic in the pit of my stomach. I'm listening attentively, but I don't hear any sound coming from the other room. Are they sleeping already? Spooning? If I don't masturbate I'll never fall asleep. I try to imagine them in the wide bed of satiny blue sheets. The writer on top of Greta. She is fucking her hard, and Greta closes her eyes and opens her lips. After a little while, the writer stops, and with her hand still inside, she spits from above. The saliva falls right onto Greta's hard clitoris.

She fucks her. She rubs her. Grabbing her by the ass, she invites her to flip over and starts licking her from behind. Greta is beautiful. Now I am the one on top of her. I let myself go.

Then I make her disappear, finally.

I wake up in the middle of the night again. It is a mystery what the body can bear. There's an excess stirred by contact that can't be undone by the mere frustration of a desire: It reappears in the fantasy.

It's about making her lose verticality. With no more insistence than that of a gaze, which—after months of following her with the shyness of a dog—one day decides to be rigorous and hits the mark. I wanted the writer to collapse from her heights, wanted her to want to collapse, to remain attentive but from the ground, finally from the ground like animals.

I don't push her. I sustain her gently by the neck without even leading her direction, and she kneels on her own. The collapse occurs slowly. First in her expression: Her eyelids droop, her eyes half closing. Her mouth also collapses and opens slightly, as if her lower lip was heavier. Her tongue, heavy in her mouth; the saliva—

saliva weighing on and beneath her tongue—accumulating in the sides of her mouth. The collapse moistens her and prepares her, while her legs fold and she's left on her knees.

I stroke her lips with my thumb, and I hold her by the chin. I go bit by bit, impatient. She surrenders herself too quickly, and I pull away. I want to be the one who opens her mouth by lunging inside it.

I tell her, "Let's wait." I hold her face by the jaw. I lean forward and meet her where she is. Both of us on the ground, but she at my will. I open her up again with my thumb. She offers up her tongue, and I spit inside her mouth. She receives it with no surprise, holds it for a few seconds, and then swallows.

That is the image that detonates me: She gathers the bits of saliva from her lips with the tip of her tongue. She doesn't close her eyes. She doesn't close them when she kisses, and I understand she won't when she's sucking. She wants to see it all, even beyond all possible perspective. She wants to see herself from the outside, slurping, rhythmic. Being something that is mine.

Her face held still, I'm going to enter her just a little. Her soft lips and her mouth are filling with more and more saliva. I stick my fingers in and out a few centimeters, but so quickly that she can't react, and she relaxes her entire expression, not trying to move. Stroking her face, I push my fingertips against her cheek: The index and middle fingers gently touch her from inside while the thumb strokes the skin of her face. Then, I place my hand in the middle and move it slowly in circles, filling her entirely.

I see the nakedness of her shoulders, collarbone, and chest. I want to feel her tits against me. I hold them. Moving faster now, in and out, I push her tongue down. She can barely move but slightly matches my movements with her neck. I tell her, "You're a bitch—is that what you wanted to hear? Your inflexibility drives me to despair, your distance drives me to despair, and now I can make my way into your throat, and you want to sustain me. I can keep filling your mouth with one hand while the other pulls aside your wet panties and fucks you suddenly for the first time. You don't want me to ask for permission, do you? That's the whole point. You are never going to close your eyes. Not even if I do it harder, like this. You want to look; you want to see me be capable of doing what I desire. Be capable of putting my desire for you above all the things that intimidate and frighten me."

To reach her desire I have to be capable of writing a story. Of playing with stories. Stories are filled with roles, with the past, with tension. I'm not intimidated by writing. Isn't it something we do all the time? Imagine, build scenarios? Now I just have to do it a little more consciously. Could I someday really call her a bitch while looking into her lovely eyes, so wise and settled? Without a timid giggle coming over me, or my voice trembling? I can practice it in front of the mirror. Bitch.

What is a bitch? I see a beautiful wild dog with a tail the color of fire. Intelligent, proud, elusive. Attacking the corral by night, emerging with a quail in its jaws; innocent, compelled by hunger and the fair right to study all the prey before taking what she needs. Not one more bird and not one less. The exact focus, the hunt without fright, without pain. She will not damage the rest; she will focus her pupil on one, and she will be exacting with her bite.

Now, I believe, it must be me. One among many—the herbivore who stopped in the middle of the field, among the remains of hay and split grain. Discovered, surprised, I will begin to run when she is too close and it is already too late, with her profile etched on my cornea. The seduction: that theatrical race where no one chases and no one flees, not violent nor painful, just the two of us converging in the race, intoxicated in the same movement of various poses. Calm in the tenderness, knowing that sharp teeth will graze the neck but harm nothing, that the jaw will not clamp down because, although it can be used for the hunt, it is also used to carry her only pup, the most beloved.

A bitch that runs with her quail in her mouth, carries it to a clearing in the forest, comforts and licks it amid the fallen leaves, watches in surprise as the bird's feathers change to a mammal's dense fur. It grows fangs and increases in size by ten, so that the bitch is suddenly between the paws of a large canine who looks at her harshly for a few seconds before dropping down on its back, asking to be pet. The bitch now has an animal in her paws as carnivorous as herself, although also as milk-suckled, as nurtured as she among warm teats, as much of a hunter as a daughter who licks, who demands, seeks out and also fears the authority of her mother.

If I could tell her a story—with the voice of the morning, bringing it to her ear, waking up together—I would tell her this one.

Didn't she say that we women had been denied the legacy of our own myths and that's why we don't have the words to explain our love?

"Tell me, tell me, tell me," she would ask, her voice losing patience amid the sheets, when she was already beginning to wake up. "Tell me more. Is this story real?"

A single ray of morning sunlight entering through the picture windows. A hand that opens to show her one small, brown quail feather. That is the proof—*look, look, look*. Proof of the obstinate and exhausting race we ran together, until we were transformed and drained.

Neither of us was harmed, and if we ever lost strength, together we recouped it in spades.

I want to enter her from behind, little by little. For her to remain still and surprised. For me to remain still and surprised. Both of us like that, united by the desire to transgress limits.

She licks my mouth very slowly; my mouth doesn't move, and she is nursing on my lips with her weight resting on me, her long hair falling on my chest—the scent of her breath, the vapor that forms from the mingling of our exhalations.

And if she takes me, serious, looking straight at me, with the calm expression of someone who knows what she's doing and doesn't need to flaunt it, then I will use the little girl voice, the small moan, and I will twist and open myself beneath her arms.

6.

As she rests the groceries on the kitchen counter, several shiny plums roll out and fall into the stone tub that forms the sink. Unsurprised, she lets them roll and opens the tap so its flow washes the fruit. She acts naturally; her way of moving, generating small scenes I can't photograph, keeps me expectant.

She speaks: "Good morning, beautiful."

Does she say that to everyone?

She and I, alone again. More than ever, I want to ask her two things: What does she have with Greta, and what is she looking for in me? Yet I don't feel I have the right to put her privacy in a crossroads of words. Or perhaps that's an excuse and I'm just afraid of the answer.

An incorrect response would ruin my freedom to continue fantasizing.

There is a pleasure in fantasy that we don't always appreciate. However, because I've decided to stay in this house, trapped in this time of tension and waiting, I feel that I am beginning to face my own desire. Perhaps I will never comprehend what moves the other, but I am a little closer to understanding what moves me.

I read in one of her books that fantasy is the response to the question "What does the other want?" Girls fantasize when, as they wonder about the love of the other—"What does Mamá want?"—they can no longer answer with certainty: "She wants me." Something has interfered between love and the mother, so a shadow both distressing and seductive appears that suggests the mother is someone beyond her love for her daughter, an other whose independence is also frightening, for it has the ability to hurt.

In the little girl's fantasy, she rehearses possible scenarios where her mother rejects her and chooses her. *What does the other want? Who do I have to be for the other to want me?* Imagine it, test out the gesture, fake it, practice it. The girl, in silence, is a great film director. The only child, a great seductress. As an only child, she seems to be closer to capturing her mother's total desire. Only a man, or the idea of a man, occasionally stands in the way.

What does he have that she wants?

Look, look, I have it, too, Mamá.

In my hands it glimmers with greater intelligence; it is sweetness, Mamá.

◆ ◆ ◆ ◆

More books open on the dining room table, a quote from Roland Barthes's *A Lover's Discourse: Fragments*:

> *I perform, discreetly, lunatic chores; I am the sole witness of my lunacy. What love lays bare in me is* energy.

I am also that lunatic who fantasizes scenarios and never shares them. One who loves, hates, envies, who could feel guilty for it, and yet I know that there is something in me that isn't all bad.

I'm still childish: I offer up my life with innocence.

She, on her knees on the kitchen floor, holding the dog's head while she stares into one of her eyes. The image is strange: A woman's body peering at the eye of an unmoving wolf, who consents to her proximity. Part of her long, tangled hair is inside her T-shirt and the other part falls forward, covering her cheek. Her feet, with short, round toes, leave a little cloud of steam on the enameled ceramic floor. I had never noticed before that she's missing a bit of her left thumbnail, which seems to have been gone for years.

The dog woke up with one eye covered in green mucus, and the writer is studying the dog's tear duct, moving the skin around it until she finds a reddened little lump.

"It's infected. The connective tissue is inflamed, you see? This always happens to her, ever since she was a puppy. It happens when she travels or when there are changes in her environment.

She doesn't seem to be in pain, but she's just putting on a brave face. The vet will want to prescribe antibiotics again. But it's better to wash it with an infusion of flowers a few times and see how it progresses. Nurse, I need your help. Stay with her and keep her calm while I go boil the flowers."

I ask what kind of flowers, and I don't ask the other question that is worrying me more. If the dog is in her own house and, apart from our short trip, her routine seems untarnished, what change in her environment has brought this on? Was she suggesting that my presence upsets her dog? Will that conversation be the beginning of another, where she asks me to go back to Barcelona?

"Chamomile, of course; a classic for conjunctivitis," she replies as she empties a jar of yellow balls into a red saucepan of boiling water. Then she comes over to us with a yellow cushion in her hand, which she drops onto the floor. "Get comfortable. It still has to sit and cool off before we can apply it." She often speaks in the plural to refer to actions she mostly carries out herself. In that plural, my role becomes important. Holding the dog by her collar, stroking her behind the ears, making sure she doesn't leave or try to scratch herself.

After straining the liquid and placing it in a green mug, she pulls out a piece of white gauze from a small cabinet and immerses it in the infusion. Leaning toward us, she begins to clean the dog's eye with the wet gauze, so all of the mucus film covering her eyelid starts to come unstuck.

She doesn't show any single sign of disgust. She is a caretaker. She must have also taken care of her mother, in some way or another. Why so much guilt?

✦ ✦ ✦ ✦

"It's been a long time since you tried to take a photo. Don't you have something you need to hand in?"

"The assignment, the photographs for the book," I said. "I didn't accept it because I was interested in the work itself, but because I wanted to be your guest; be your guest, and then give it to you as a gift."

"Give me what?" she asks, smiling slightly with just one side of her mouth, the curve at the bottom, beneath the gentle cleft of a dimple.

"The book."

"Huh, really? That was it."

She carried something hidden in her fist that the dog was licking, trying to get her to open her fingers.

The swaying motion of her steps reminds me of an image, when I noticed her entire body for the first time as she stepped off the train. Her slenderness and the strength of her legs impressed me. Could a woman with slender legs some day love me? Although others already had, every encounter between a body like that and mine opened up a new insecurity.

A body like that. The silhouette seen from behind, with her bare ankle resting on a low heel. I speak of the definition of a bone beneath the skin. What does it mean? A body capable of being moved, lifted in arms. An aspirational ankle, that's what we were taught . . .

I think that, in her gestures, she isn't that different from those slight, smiling, and sometimes cruel girls. The girls who choose and spurn their girlfriends, but at the same time are brutally chosen and rejected by boys.

Her elegance: perhaps an iron rod that goes through her back and that her body has come to recognize as part of itself. It is surrounded by a field of tissue. In the end it is flexible, like a reed.

Today I spent several hours in the sun in the garden and my skin dried out, and a few wrinkles on my forehead appear more pronounced. When I enter the house and look in the bathroom mirror, my left eye also seems more irritated than ever.

Fear of the monster I will be tomorrow. Will I have surgery one day so they can love me when my entire eyeball is covered by a glitter of bloodied cells? Or will I put ruby red makeup on my eyelids and dark circles, searching for another bright color that combines with my own, like a lovely mask. My face like that of a salamander.

I look at the dog's eye, already cured of its infection. I compare it with mine.

As a woman, I am a foreign body; I've always known that. Even just the word *woman* awakens a voluptuousness that makes me uncomfortable if it is applied to me. Yet, she . . . her appeal is also the conversation that her beauty maintains with the norm. Neither within nor outside of it. A powerful, arrogant, disrespectful conversation. If someone might consider her ugly, then her ugliness would just become an aesthetic inspiration. Her position is always in the center; her presence makes everything around her light up or pale, according to her will.

The straight nose; the sad gaze.

I make myself a coffee at ten in the morning. I had a lot of trouble getting out of bed after a night of broken sleep.

She must have gone out to the beach with the dog much earlier. On the kitchen table, she left a mug with a bit of coffee remnants and a plate stained with oil, with some crumbs and seeds. There is also a black pen from a New York hotel and a small notebook. These are the first signs of her work that I've seen in days. I start to think that perhaps the reason for that slight dejection in her character is that she's not writing, that she can't write.

I think that opening the notebook isn't an assault on her privacy but rather a gesture of self-protection. I need to know what sort of relationship, with what sort of person, I am becoming caught up in. If I can understand what she feels, I imagine I will be able to act in the most practical way possible.

The handwriting is lengthy and irregular, but perfectly legible. One always wonders if private things "forgotten" where prying eyes will find them are not simply letters with a clearly intended recipient. As far as I know, she isn't expecting any visitors today. I must be the recipient.

Is it possible to be together at the wrong time?

Live together and even still do so preserving a temporal distance as truncation:

To not be together in the time of desire. Of affection. Or of the spirit.

With the recurrence of moments where synchronicity failed, an irreparable distance is built. I know that from before.

Out of sync with the other: How much can a body bear without giving up hope? Is the experience of asynchronism an event that generates detachment and rupture, or are all relationships naturally "out of sync"?

We never reach joy at the same time because our wounds have different natures. It is obvious, two animals wounded by two different pains, yet their pains both affect their ability to surrender. They truncate it.

When eros does not find its path, but the context suggests seduction, each one will wait in silence for the other to attack first.

If I could break into sobs, shriek to obliterate the tense order, would I receive your passion?

Other times in the past they've observed me from outside as I sobbed like a nursling, without understanding that my sobs were always sobs of love.

I remember the fascist rigidness of someone who did not feel and could not show up for me. There is no compassion if the body is not moved. I don't want that to happen again. How do we run the risk of finding a lack of compassion in those we choose?

Anguish: The body thinks that the only way it can survive is by repairing the bond of damaged love.

I don't understand the text because I don't understand my place in the discourse. I could be inside, be the other, or be outside. Not have a place in her writing, because I don't have a place in her desire.

It seems a stolen notebook reveals nothing; it merely serves to confuse.

I am here. One inexorably heads toward the encounter with her own story.

I feed on the information I've been stealing. Hunger for knowledge. I read her books from the living room shelves. If I know what she knows, perhaps I will eventually understand her. I read much more than she reads. My mental voice has changed its tone due to the texts and their musicality. There is a narration inside my head. I observe what is happening and the voice narrates and accompanies my silence. The voice inside, the mouth tightly closed.

Sometimes I'm critical. I judge her apparent lack of productivity. Perhaps she worked before and no longer does. Sometimes I get angry over that hedonism through which she directs her energy to nowhere I'm familiar with. It makes me angry, how she looks out into the void, locks herself in her mind. Also the pleasure she gets from pampering her dog. As I wait for the materialization of my desire, I observe how I'm progressively swamped by worse feelings.

Who does she fuck? How does she do it? Why am I so obsessed by these questions? Because she decided for me that I don't need to know. Her silence, and perhaps this is the simplest answer, is due to my being here. Watching. Fascinated by her privacy. Interrupting the normal flow of this house.

A red evening. Red as few are.

We see the sunset from the promenade, where the row of houses faces the sea. September is ending, and only a few tourists dine on outdoor tables. We order squid with baby favas, potato salad, and smoked sardine. They serve half of a single sardine naked on an enormous slice of bread rubbed with tomato. It is so alone that the result is comical.

I adore you, ma'am. We've been drinking. I hear it in my own voice, repeated over and over again inside my head as we laughed together. I do not say it out loud.

Surely she doesn't love, or at least not passionately, because she doesn't do the things that people in love do around those who unsettle them.

What does a person who loves do? What are the gestures of a "normal" lover?

I can't help but ask myself a series of inappropriate questions, over and over again. Their approach is appalling, but I want to use them as a mold to measure my luck or my misfortune. I choose to formulate the wrong question, which points to an exhausting tongue twister destined to lead me down a dead end. I know it. I am not moved by respect for the other's different reality but by rage, resentment that is born of dissatisfaction. I tell my sex to shut up. I tell my character not to be broken, self-esteem damaged since birth.

I don't wear dresses; I'm not flirty. The wound of not being enough is my gender marker. I wear it in secret—I would do anything to be the chosen one. Beneath neutral clothing I carry a sex that cries like a wounded ego. It is not loved. No. Who could mistake this indifference for love?

I move through the house on tiptoes. I gather up all my objects from the bathroom so they aren't too visible. I do not want my presence in her space to be excessive, but rather lacking so she will demand it, realizing the distance that I, too, can impose. Tonight, after dinner, it seems she wants to linger and chat. For me to stay there with her, sitting in the kitchen.

When she speaks, she brings her open palms to her neck. Protecting it. Cradling her voice. Her intelligent and sad gaze drops. She clenches her jaw subtly and looks suspiciously at the camera that hangs on my chair, out of its case. I will not touch it.

Apathy. After frustration and sadness comes apathy.

A passion settled in despair.

In apathy, one no longer desires the other but ends up desiring that newly conquered heroism: calmness in dissatisfaction.

7.

Notebook

Who am I beyond the living memory of a girl without a home? Who, like a thief, after her mother's death, had three hours to empty out the space where the family had lived before it was closed up. Accompanied by three strange men with their packing gear. The closets illuminated by candles because they had cut off the electricity.

How can I explain to her, or simply how can I remind her, that the adult body does not get over some things?

The loss of the primary, the obligatory structuring: Papá, Mamá, home. The first debacle that proves that everything in life, even what is most ours, is susceptible to devastation.

A bond damaged by routine violence in the family space. A sick mother. A father crushed by a sick mother. Who he no longer loves. Doesn't want to take care of. Even look at.

The father moves to another country. He starts to speak another language. He is reborn many miles away. He changes completely, and yet, when he falls in love again, it is with a very similar woman. He has another child, a son. Little by little he cuts off contact with his daughter. He manages to do so delicately, through small acts of forgetfulness. A daughter who reminds him too much of that first wife. Of the passion and the terror she produced in him. Death in life.

The little girl wants to cover her eyes and not see them. Not see her mother both nesting and burning the house down from the inside. Loving and abusing her family. Dinnertime, wine, shouting. The mother knows that she is dying. The doctors have told her. But she is still alive. She can't stand being alive far from the father who no longer cares about her life. Or cares too much. So much that he flees, is incapable of living in the same country.

Anne Dufourmantelle writes in *En cas d'amour: Psychopathologie de la vie amoreuse*:

> *Even when two parents tear each other apart, they don't always make sad children. Indeed, children cannot afford that luxury; they are too busy supporting their parents and trying to meet their expectations, making them believe that life is possible and worthwhile. They are exemplary, small soldiers standing tall in their boots, light weapons in their fists, and their eyes firmly on the horizon, constantly alert. They don't sleep much, they cry very little, and they never complain.*

After many years that relationship collapses. And, in fact, it isn't a catastrophic ending; it's caused by erosion, by exhaustion. One fine day, when I no longer fear loss—because it has always been savagely lying in wait—I buy a house behind her back. I start to be absent many evenings, busy with the renovation. That is how she comes to accuse me of having a lover. I do not have a lover, but I do have a secret. And in that moment, I am learning for the first time in my life that I have the right to my own privacy. In other words, the right to not tell everything, to not confess. A house and my own privacy when I'm already in my forties. An independence achieved progressively. An inheritance I give myself.

One day I adopt a dog. And that's something I can't hide. Because with the dog I begin to desire. Specifically, I desire to not be separated from the puppy. The following day, the puppy and I move into the house, without luggage. I send a moving company to the other house to gather up my things. I learned that from my father: to not keep returning in body when what one needs to do is leave.

> *We are made of the texture of ghosts; our lineage is made of them and the others: fleeting encounters, dreams, possibilities, missed connections, hopes. Our ghosts know better than us what we have given up. Being bathed in war [. . .] means that we cannot even offer ourselves in love nor lose ourselves in it, only try to hold on to the fragile territory we kept from violence.*

I could tell you all this, girl, so you would understand. But why poison your life with mine? Besides, you never ask questions. It is important to respect the desire not to know.

At no point has she tried to touch me in a clear advance. I won't be the one to do it; because of our age difference, it's only fair that she demonstrate her will, ask for it. She has to be sure. She has to say it clearly. She has to continue the hand stroking from the car, since that in itself is not enough. I need her to be the one who puts forth her will, articulates it. Even more than once, even more than twice.

If I were the one who took the first step, if I took it as a leap into the void and her body retreated gloomily, or worse, if she remained stock-still and accepted the kiss or even returned it due to the pressure of living in my house, or the strange influence of my name: How could I ever get over the horror of having put my desire ahead of her will?

Go too far if you want to. Let me spoil you with my years. Be awkward inside me; be bold, fickle; be even a tyrannical hungry girl, but be hungry for flesh, not for images to sell to others.

From the Latin *seducere*, formed by the separable prefix *se-* and the verb *ducere* (to lead). *Ducere* comes from the Indo-European root **deuk-*, which means lead, direct, and maneuver.

Isn't it possible to think of a meaning for seduction that has no negative connotations? A seduction that doesn't imply power games, a negative distancing from one's origin toward the interests of another. The way I'm thinking about it, seduction means a displacement of one person toward the other that constitutes a third space: the space of the two of us together. We are no longer you nor me, not your story nor mine, but the flexible mesh of a new fabric, the warp of each of our previous histories before the meeting that braided us together. That's what I want: together sustaining the strands until the limits dissolve, until the strands of the braid are tangled with no logic of combined units, blending purely out of passion and intuition.

I am trying to defend, for myself, a meaning of seduction that brings the rituals of guiding, of leading, toward us each being able to move individually to a third place of shared intimacy.

One needs desire to reach intimacy, but most of all one needs time, coexistence, to be exposed to the other's presence. Do I have to tell her that this is what I was seeking when I invited her to spend the end of the summer with me? But if a plan of seduction is confessed, does it cease to be a seduction? I would interrupt the mystery of desire for the other. It would be like forcing her to participate in my narrative of what is happening between us, when perhaps hers is very different... What does she want from me? A few images? Then the risk of finally watching her leave, like a stranger, with a folder of photographs under one arm. Watching her leave this house, my privacy plundered, rushing—typical of someone her age—to live some new experiences. One protects herself in seduction because she doesn't yet know what the other wishes. How could she if she hasn't even had time to comprehend her own? Everything happens so fast in the beginning, it's so unreliable . . . I'm sad over an old love that failed. I can't risk having her come today with her sparkle, only to not even be able to hold my gaze tomorrow because she no longer feels the same.

Sometimes she seems serious, elusive, refusing to speak to me when we pass each other in the hallway, and it's as if she doesn't have a clue. Or at least she hasn't realized that it's a question of time. One needs time for the seduction to progress and for desire to file down the rough edges of difference. To prepare us to fall together, one on top of the other, like two river stones. I almost trust in it, but not yet. I feel distanced from her by the hero worship—I'm not sure if that's a generational thing. I'm shocked that, when she arrived, she thought that after two days together she would already have access to all of me. And then what: A photograph awkwardly posted online, communicating something, when we still have so much work to do? The work of seduction, of writing.

When I was her age, thirty, I had incipient cervical cancer. They tried to eliminate it in various ways and nothing worked. I began to lose patience and suffer. I wanted them to remove the entire organ, the possibility, the waiting. "But you don't have any children yet, you're still young," the doctors, male and female, would repeat indifferently when looking at my file. "It could affect you, you know? Psychologically. Many women feel they're somehow no longer women."

What is affecting me psychologically is that you are punishing me, leaving something inside me that could kill me. Because you've decided that a woman is a breeding sack. What is it to be a woman? It is the materialization of a belief. And I don't believe. "What if you change your mind and want to have a baby later?" I've always rejected the idea, and now, with the pronouncement of a potential death inside of me, one so similar to my mother's, and my uterus chained to identity, the thought of conceiving a human body made me feel only rage, repulsion.

I was maternal, sure, just like I am now. With all sorts of

animals; young kids and slow old people. I take care of them with my whole body. Is that being maternal? Lovingly cleaning up my dog's feces and vomit. Sleeping on a bed filled with small shed hair. Accepting her constant interruptions into my work time eagerly, with no anger. When she was a puppy, I wanted to see her grow up. And when she's an old lady, I will hope for a life without pain for her. Her well-being is the most important thing to me. And I employ my body, immediately, to achieve it.

I wasn't there for my mother to the very end. Our conflict was too great. She hadn't been good to me; her envy wouldn't allow her to be. I was afraid of seeing her changed face. I was afraid of her face, but not for the first time. I'd always feared it; its rage, its taut expression that foretold problems. Yet I mothered my girlfriends. My girlfriends, regardless of their sex. I listened to them speak with the shrill voice of a sparrow hatchling demanding, in an obscenely visible manner, with its beak open. I never had intimacy with men, and my father lives in another country. I didn't come into this world to support men or teach them anything. Everyone has to secretly know their own purpose. What they want to take from me, it won't be in my house, but from afar, in writing.

Who still wants to be called "a normal man"? If they'd given me that suit at birth, I would have ripped it off myself and crawled over to the others, those who no longer wore it, seeking refuge.

We aren't pretty, in the common meaning of the word, but beauty overflowers wherever we are. That reality does not escape me. It is indisputable. The space we occupy together contracts, spasms, satisfies itself. Although our aesthetic is austere and we dress in simple cuts and muted colors, our presence in the space revolutionizes it; it is a luxury that makes the wisteria in the garden bloom, full and powerfully scented.

I contemplate the young photographer. I see her leave her room. I think the narrative of love already sustains us. I tell her, "Good morning, beautiful," and I'm the one who feels a shock of pleasure travel from my belly to my chest. Even though she is the one who is surprised by the words, which leave her unsettled yet motionless.

"Good morning, beautiful." She gets nervous, tries to understand whether that's something one says to a young girl, to a friend, or to a lover. If she were to ask me, if she finally dared to ask me directly, I would tell her, *Don't worry, darling, we are all of those things*.

I'm so fortunate now. I have a young woman in my house, loose-haired, slow only at dawn, to whom I can say "Good morning, beautiful."

Soon I will kiss her, after the morning greeting. It will be natural by now. Today I delight in the moments prior to that happening. I hope she doesn't suffer in the wait; I hope she, too, can enjoy this anticipation.

8.

The writer is absent, on a work trip. Ten days. Soon I will go to Barcelona, so Greta is staying to take care of the dog and water the plants.

She wears her jeans with that elastic, tight fit. Without the writer around, her beauty is a luxurious, excessive gift. I can look at her.

Standing beside my desk—where the tall vase and sunflowers rest—Greta, a long scarf with green stripes around her neck, inspects one of the simpler cameras, a 35mm point and shoot with a plastic lens.

"Almost a toy," I tell her. "But the light from the window, the yellow of the sunflowers, and the texture of the lock of hair trapped beneath the olive-green scarf, all of that is working in our favor."

She holds my gaze for the photograph. She doesn't seem worried about how long I take to shoot, because her eyes don't change and she smiles several times. It's a lot, her mouth. I imagine how it might look: her upper lip slightly elevated because her left incisor is large and slightly overlaps the right one.

She forgot to take off her sneakers and walks through the living room holding a slice of cheese in front of the dog's snout, who follows her. The writer does not allow street shoes inside her home.

"You forgot to leave your sneakers by the door," I tell her, and Greta brings her hand to her mouth, makes a shocked expression, and then shrugs.

"Once doesn't count."

She's sat on my lap on the sofa and laughs; she laughs so hard she cries. She was trying to open a bottle of wine with a knife and the cork slipped inside, splattering wine everywhere: her hair, her face, my shirt, and the wall. Before she got so close, she used her shirt to wipe the wine off the white wall, and I pretended to be shocked at all the craziness and erratic behavior.

We are similar in how we seek out calm. Our urgency to drink as soon as we were left alone in the house. The computer playing a television dating show. Hummus straight from the container. A bag of popcorn.

She is gentle atop me; it is easy. At first she was rushing, but now she slowly lets herself be kissed.

I remember what it was like: to be willing to sacrifice anything for this sensation. I am going to enter her mouth.

I am entering her mouth.

A memory of inebriation. I've experienced it before, but it feels like the first time: kissing.

I want for nothing; all is pure sweetness.

I tell myself that this, and not rage or jealousy, is my natural place.

"There was no way of knowing you were so fun. If I had to judge from the time the three of us spent together, I would've said you were nursing some wounded heart, like some dark emo chick—the kind of person who has a past still echoing through her like a thunderstorm. Like your girlfriend from first grade dumped you for a boy who drew better crayon dinosaurs, and you never got over it. From then on it was all resentment and darkness, despite your obvious intelligence and a sweetness that surfaces every once in a while. I'm not particularly drawn to cryptic energy, but in your case, there's a slight 'angry child' vibe that turns me on."

She squirts lotion onto her fingertips and spreads it around her eyelids. She undoes a small bun on her nape and untangles her hair as she looks into the mirror and tells me about the last time she heard Ángeles Toledano sing in Seville. "I love, love, love her. You know this song, when she sings to the saeta singers?"

She sings softly about blind singers on a green night, leaving behind the burning traces of love. She applies Vaseline to her lips. All those gestures. Her delicacy, the absolute pleasure in being able to look at a woman.

She sits on the bidet and washes herself with warm water.

She's left the bathroom door open and talks to me from inside. I observe her from the bed.

Joy, joy, joy.

Intimacy is the body. A mystery that cannot be solved with the words of this world.

I wake up next to her, and it has already happened. Was it the dinner and conversation? No, then we were still two people with separate stories and intentions, although soon we would understand each other well.

The intimacy came later, in a delicate combination of sex and language. The few words she spoke yesterday protected me in a sheath of solid, constant desire: "I want this; I'm asking for it; I enjoy it." Naming the smell. The taste. *Am I going too fast?* Doesn't matter, it's true; I'm quick, so is Greta.

My water breaks and she licks. She says I'm soft inside. That it feels like the velvet that covers certain fruits. That they've tried to hide the existence of that softness from women who spend half their lives with men. "You can't know yourself this way; you have to be inside another woman." She says that she could also, if need be, die to make a place like that hers. That she would stain it if her body was capable of creating a thick fluid with which to do so. That her desires to fill that place are fierce, that instinct and imagination merge indistinguishably in such desire.

She says she wouldn't mind arriving inside, then for the lights to go out and for that to be the end.

I'm starting to love someone who's said she enjoys having me in her mouth. She speaks those words, and I start to love her as she's saying them. "That's what I want from you: the smell, the taste. I love it. I chase it. I could stay there in it, or leave for just a second and then dive back in." Sometimes we need our experiences to be completed by small affirmations that allow us to interpret them with some confidence.

Because she wants me, I can lower my guard and turn my back and relax my sphincter beneath her pressing fingers. I can come in her mouth and then kiss her again.

Naked beside her, my body seems normal. There are no major differences between her size and mine. That similarity protects me.

Intimacy is the kind of surrender we encountered. We are shocked when repulsion is no longer possible and there is only voraciousness, gluttony. The body knows itself desired, then it offers up sweat, saliva. Our thighs, our bellies, our hips fit together. Feeling the buttocks, holding it up. A spiral that constantly returns to its point of origin.

✦ ✦ ✦ ✦

The generosity of the sex enthralls the body that sleeps and kisses at the same time. Sleepwalking snakes shaking their rattles, moving them just a little, just as the abdomen rises and lowers with each breath. Now I remember us and see us, from the impossible perspective of the room's ceiling, like two coiled snakes. Two rattles trembling at the end of two tubular bodies that embrace and contort. I, too, would open my mouth to receive the venom, and if she spat it inside me, it couldn't harm me. A liquor, we would drink it.

And I wonder if we are miserable here alone, biting into the beauty of this house, using as we wish the fantasy that the writer created over so much time and with so much care. Because I inevitably feel that there is something bad in those minutes, those hours where we are better without her because being without her makes us more free to look into each other's eyes, to laugh. Perhaps we are taking advantage because being here, using her things, spilling wine—and making a joke of it and cracking up—we forget about her. Are we forgetting? I wonder which of the two of us finds it easier to leave her out, if we achieve it effortlessly thanks to desire, or whether "third wheel" is forever inscribed between Greta and me and, therefore, our existing beyond the writer is an act of justice. To feel that we, too, are defining the rules of this game; that we've taken stock of the story and we are all three equal co-creators: the same eagerness and willingness to seek out beauty, the same vulnerability, and the same fear of abandonment.

Greta is outside, sunbathing, wrapped in a white bath towel. The dog follows me everywhere and, out in the garden, she remains glued to my leg. Would she be capable of coming to Barcelona with me rather than staying in her own house with Greta?

I say, "Greta, darling, thank you for these two days. You've saved me from something."

I say that I don't want to go, *no, no, no*. I say that it's a shame, but I promised I'd be in Barcelona for the birthday of one of my housemates. I suspect she knows I'm such a coward that I could never stick around, waiting for the other woman to return, welcoming her after how Greta and I have sabotaged her habits, desecrated her small temple.

I don't know if what we've done is right or wrong. I don't know if the writer will care. I try to imagine her first expression, our next gaze.

I can't leave the night when the day comes. I can't even remotely try.

Once back in the city, I slept, showered, ate, drank, and spoke with people on the street and on the phone. The memory prevailed.

What to do with the heat? With the lingering energy?

The next day and the next, like licking the golden wrappers left in an empty box of chocolates.

◆ ◆ ◆ ◆

My own urgency in pleasure and her voice calming me: "Take it slow. No one's going to take it away from you. It's yours, *mamita*, relax."

Even though I think I'm the only one who fears shattering every day, while we were doing it, I went to the bathroom to drink water and wash my hands. I observed myself in the mirror. My image was much more friendly than when I'd looked at myself that morning. My face no longer seemed angular, disproportionate. The direction of my eyes was somewhat more symmetrical. My skin was ruddy and, in general, looked healthy.

Remembering scenes suddenly opens my belly with a hot whiplash. Later, in the opposite direction, sometimes I distance myself, and the guilt overwhelms me.

I recall a conversation with the writer the night before she left. She sounded sad: "It's not that I don't want to talk, it's that over time I've grown more silent. I used to believe that speaking was what I should do, what people expected of me in a casual meeting; to share reflections, stories. Later, as things started to go better for me, I began to feel that my words took on an aura of authority that made me seem pedantic and attention-seeking. I saw how the person who supposedly loved me wanted me to shut up, wanted to not have to listen to my voice over the others at a table. I was repulsed by my reflection in her eyes. I decided to change, although it was hard at first: Speaking with no filters was what I'd been doing my entire life. I was happy when talking. In that period I also began to look into the mirror and feel that I had aged. My skin had detached from its anchorage points and my expression was different. I always looked tired. So I thought that, all of a sudden, I'd lost my freedom to speak and my youth. It made a lot of sense that those two things happened at the same time. All women are tormented by our reflection at some point. We rejoin the others, subdued and muted by the shock of seeing ourselves through our worst eyes."

9.

Notebook

It is an exhausting work trip. One city, another, then another. The kindness of friends I see year after year. An airplane, two trains, and the night in a histrionic hotel whose piped-in music I can't manage to turn off. I call the reception desk: "The music is part of the personality of the chain; it's at the disposal of the guest, just like the pillow menu." I consider sending a message to the girls and asking them how it's going, but I don't want to seem controlling, or much worse, maternal. I try to write. I order a soup for supper and make decaf coffee in the machine. Then I grab a tonic water from the little fridge. Will I sleep tonight? That's a crapshoot on every travel day. At what time will I be woken up by some parent shouting at their kids on the way to the breakfast buffet? Why do they get up so early for breakfast? Good grief.

I open up Instagram and, over a few long minutes, look at animal videos. I cry over a poodle who has slept on his owner's grave every time they take him to visit her at the cemetery for the last four years. I miss my dog so much. I hate not bringing her with me. Is she upset that I'm not there?

I want to ask the girls if she's okay, but I know I shouldn't. Would it seem like an excuse? I miss her paw on my knee begging for soup, almost scratching me with her insistence. Pulling her up onto the bed, even though it's not allowed and hotels always place a cushion on the floor as an alternative. Watching her sink her snout into the spongy white sheets.

Spending time in hotels always reminds me of that three-month residency I spent in Italy, before we broke up. Yes, it is true I often think of that time. Feeling miserable in a perfect landscape is something that's hard to forget. Beautiful cities bewitch us when we experience them without love. Like in the song "Que c'est triste Venise." It sounds corny, I know. Songs about heartbreak are grotesque to those who aren't feeling it. The expression of others' pain is somewhat obscene for those living with optimism, but optimism . . . isn't my strong suit. Even still, I get embarrassed, of course. Of the possibility of being stereotypical: the writer quoting a Charles Aznavour song in a language she doesn't even speak. That's what you call me, "the writer." And I like that because it makes me just an ordinary writer. An ordinary writer is considered "too intense" in conversation. She's the subject of private mockery, sometimes affectionate mockery, I like to think.

That's why most of the time I prefer to keep silent and wait for the page . . . On paper emotions are digested differently because readers read alone, approach the text in search of answers, a conversation and, as such, are willing to play by the rules. If the reader enters the text, they have entered a ritual time where the type of judgment that could make me seem ridiculous in a conversation is suspended.

For a while at that residency I was homesick and missed my partner, whom I imagined with other women. We could say I didn't take full advantage of the trip, living physically somewhere different from where my body was. One day on my way to the library, I stood staring at a recently built church, with a contemporary architectural style but maintaining the Christian motifs: a large iron cross, a body with wounds, a mother with her arms open awaiting her son. I realized the door was made of glass and opened automatically, like one in a supermarket. The space, vaguely modernist, was largely empty and had some central wooden images, lit up in reds and blues. I walked toward the candles—which weren't made of wax but rather some sort of little gas lamps with a glass tube and a wick—and I lit one. Then, I leaned back in a spot in front of a side altar.

I was alone, so I sang. I sang the Hail Mary the way we used to in school, one day a year, for the dawn rosary. Afterward we would have thick hot chocolate and churros for breakfast with some of the teachers, mothers, and classmates. Since we'd gotten up early, those of us who sang the dawn rosary were allowed to start school a bit later.

God, love, and guilt were the center of my girlhood education. I no longer believe in God, but back then I needed that song that emerged from my mouth and that had been sung many times along with my mother and my grandmother. Praying together, eating churros, an inexplicable joy amid the things of being a woman. Carrying a rosary in my hand and letting its little beads pass through my fingers. Their concrete feel varied depending on the material. Some heavier, some plastic. Rough or slippery. Always ending with a medal of the Virgin, who I remember depicted with a childish face, as if kindness could make us retain a girl's appearance. Not just any girl, of course, but an infant who maintains a calm and innocence that . . . I'm going too far. I was referring to the power of the oldest rituals of spirituality, which are present in the moment when consciousness is configured.

My stay in Italy wasn't long, but when I returned, her routine in Barcelona was already different without me. She had changed while I, melancholic, had suspended life, as some widows do when they manage to freeze desire in the same place as loss, around the narrative of some past time. Finding her so different, so jealously guarding her privacy in our shared home, proved that what I had feared was not the result of my anxious anticipation, but of a dark intelligence whose judgments, with no need for further justification, I would be wise to accept.

Once we were together, I realized that she, who hadn't missed me and had been more entertained than ever getting together with friends and going to bars, could tolerate our cohabitation because she was absent. She was capable of making herself absent in her own body, sharing the everyday, but withholding attention and affection. In the morning, she responded so quickly to the alarm that she left the bed even before turning it off. I always stayed behind, stretched out, horizontal. I was rejected in subtle ways that were presented as "bearable" for a "healthy" person. She would say that my long periods of loneliness in the year promoting my last book had weakened my spirits, causing my excessive reactions to normal situations.

Despite having prepared our breakfast, the woman who was my partner did not speak at the table, and when I sat down, she reacted by turning on the radio. Hearing any random program, the haphazard voice of two cretins awkwardly commenting on a play, was more important than hearing our voices together, hers and mine.

Many times I tried to carry on with the proposed script. I nestled into the hypothesis that our shared partnership did not always have to be written with passion on both sides. Perhaps we'd been lied to; perhaps this was it. Later there were moments when I simply couldn't take any more. I would start to cry overwhelming, annoying sobs—involuntary and born of desperation, yet destined to disrupt the alleged balance, the false calm, that trap I felt had been set for me with utmost kindness. The trap of capital, of lovelessness, of people who get together to have a big, light-filled house and the certainty that someone of some intelligence and sensitivity will listen to you after work when things go south.

And I cried and yelled, "Fuck, can't you see we're finished, ruined, that this political correctness is disgusting—what's-her-name and so-and-so going about their routine, despising each other? Can't you see I don't believe life lasts forever?" I cried and cried, as if crying could destroy that damn shared home, blow up her composure that was making me hate her because she wasn't sensitive to all this, all this didn't affect her—the loss of love, the noxious cohabitation without desire, without the desire to converse, touch each other, nothing.

I was crying in such a way that I was hijacking her free will, her freedom; I was kidnapping her, because if she—exhausted by my intensity—walked through the door as I cried, trying to escape the situation, the aggressiveness in my body was so great that she knew I could hurt myself and destroy everything. Then, at some impasse, out of fear of that or something worse, or perhaps out of some stirring of compassion, she seemed to be regaining tenderness, a distant empathy that was sufficient to calm me enough to stop hyperventilating and make me think: *What horror have I now become? Am I degrading myself? Can the neighbors hear me?*

10.

On the way back to the home by the sea, the train braked suddenly, as if something had interrupted its trajectory. I immediately thought it was a body. First a firetruck came, and a man in uniform went on top of it and pointed a big spotlight, level with my car, onto the tracks. The night fractured by the hard brake and a beam of light. Later more firetrucks with their intermittent blue lights—two, three, four of those—and also several ambulances, police cars, all in a circle around the tracks, like a strange gathering of blinking automobiles.

Tonight there are many people focused on one who decides to end her life. Before there was probably no one, or hardly anyone. Only the desperate, brave attempt at death manages to interrupt the order of things. A beautiful "no more" read as an antisocial attack.

Through the window I watch policemen and firemen approaching with flashlights to the place where train, body, and track come together. On the other side are the annoyed passengers, sighing loudly over not reaching their destinations. A ceremony of blue-and-white lights accompanies the transition of someone leaving their life today and the rest of us are incapable of measuring up. Do I feel more worthy of witnessing this scene because I am secretly reading it as a victory?

I see it through the window, on a platform, how they remove the body. A funeral retinue in uniforms with helmets and night gear, yellow reflective bands on black to increase visibility. They carry the body while others hold up a large black sheet to try to impose some decorum on the shocking spectacle and block the gaze of the train passengers. Even still, I manage to see some white-and-pink-striped socks. I'm surprised at how calm I feel, yet complicit, as if forming part of the same resistance that recognizes the misery some lives are trapped in. I fervently hope she pulled it off, that it was too late for any technology or hero at the service of the fatherland to revert her desire, her wish to die.

An hour and a half later the vehicles are slowly leaving, until there's only one police car left, with its sirens off. The night is black again.

When I get back to her house, I will sit in the kitchen and tell the writer about it. I'm not troubled by the episode on the train, but I hope she will be afraid that I am and will somehow try to console me. I appreciate having a horrific story to entertain us enough to keep the couple of days that Greta and I spent alone from entering the conversation. The couple of red drops that can still barely be seen on the wall beside the sofa.

Sometimes I wonder if we all have those anticipatory thoughts or if they are a result of something wrong with me.

She greets me in a long nightgown and cardigan sweater, with a hug. Nothing more. "Welcome, how've you been?"

At the same time, the dog is euphoric; her wagging tail moves her hindquarters so much she almost loses her balance.

We have a calm day. After returning, I experience the privilege of living in this house very differently. The traffic on Avinguda del Paral·lel, the noise, the pollution, left behind. Everything here is cared for. She's brought a large bouquet of sunflowers and has placed it in my room.

It seems she's finally writing at a good pace. She started on her solo trip, in some hotel room. Now she continues in the house, and I enjoy the evening stroll through the rowboats. The dog runs ahead of me. I follow the prints of her pads on the damp sand.

II.

There is some peace tonight because what I was anxiously anticipating has already happened. The two of them, she and Greta, left. They went out this morning while I was sleeping, and I didn't see them leave. Greta must have arrived in her car, opened the front door, smiled with that joy that makes her seem very young, and helped her with the bags. After overhearing a phone conversation that presaged her arrival, I've spent days waiting for that scene, afraid of spending the night alone in the house and not being able to sleep. What was I most worried about? Confirming that they both wanted to share time alone together, exist beyond the perpetual guest I've become. So it was true; their bond was strong enough, had the gravity . . . to need a space where I was not. How can one live with the idea that two need each other apart from oneself? How can one accept such a reality so perfectly fair and so unbearable at the same time: not being the only one, not being anyone's favorite?

◆ ◆ ◆ ◆

My body is incapable of satisfying the needs that another might have. I remember my mother's dissatisfied face as I tried to be everything for her: a girl, a mother, a husband. Also the outrage sometimes tied to that dissatisfaction, upset to find monstrosity in her daughter—fat thighs that turn red in summer, early menstruation, sexual arousal.

I went out to dinner at the restaurant on the edge of the beach. Grilled razor clams with lemon, and two large draft beers. I wasn't hungry. I needed to maintain my vitality to keep from falling into the extra sadness endemic to extreme hunger. I wanted to get tipsy, just enough to go straight to bed after dinner.

I know what my greatest fear is. Although it may seem ridiculous, I can say it: What I most fear is my cell phone, my compulsive tendency to check WhatsApp for a message. The last one was from the writer at eleven. She wrote *Good morning* and told me they'd already left, that it was a beautiful sunny day, that I should take advantage of it. Her smug kindness irked me. Wasn't she a writer? Shouldn't she be using language in a more useful way? The first part informed me of the only thing I already knew: that they weren't in the house, that they'd gone out. Lurking behind that phrase, however, was everything I didn't know, which she refused to tell me: Where had they gone? How long were they going to be away?

I answered, friendly and succinct. Just a couple of words. If I wrote a longer message, it would reveal my sadness. And a sad body's words are always suspicious: They contain tensions, double meanings. They are violent toward the simple, utilitarian phrases of a contented body. Sadness makes creases in the language.

Her message had arrived at eleven in the morning. Later, alone before the phone screen, I experienced the abandonment over and over again. As if the silence of the screen was a face that chose to look away and avoid my eyes. A black hole that sucked my energy, yet also a space for distant hope, a port from which some day perhaps I would see the ships returning: *What's up. Thinking of you.*

I hate the feeling that everything that can happen and cannot happen has to be through the phone. But, where else if not there? I am alone, isolated. If at least they'd left me the dog . . .

I ordered a second beer and wasn't sure if the waiter's expression was one of judgment. I wanted the alcohol to make me less attentive, make me able to leave my phone in the kitchen, far from my bedroom so I couldn't confirm that neither of them had sent me a goodnight message.

The night is cool, and as I leave the restaurant, a mist is rising from the sea, weighing down the air with moisture. I cover my head with my jacket's wool hood and walk carelessly, unconcerned about a clumsy gait or figure. Solitude offers a kind of rest from seduction. No one sees me or will see me tonight. My phone burns in my pocket. What if my not checking means I'm missing a lovely message? What if I get my hopes up and check only to be plunged back into angst?

Every option opens up a chain of potential harm. How many other women around the world will find themselves tonight in a similar situation?

Many, there must be many.

Once in my bedroom I start watching the documentary the writer recommended two nights earlier with such affection and insistence.

The beauty of the images. I take notes so perhaps I can share them with her, if they come back and all goes well. *If all goes well.* What do I mean by that? That life here continues to be as good and as bad as it has been until now. That Greta wants to see me again, that the writer brings new sunflowers to my room.

The notes:

Metamorphosis of the birds. The possibility of a love, a story, a house. Eighty-four peacock feathers laid out on the ground, with their blue eyes, counted one by one by a child who fears losing his mother's caretaking. The fear at the depths of the tub at bathtime. *Give me a heart the size of a whale, that calmly submerges during storms.* A still life of squash and leeks. Sardines on newspaper and bread. Desperate sailors who imagine throwing themselves into the sea after two weeks with no letters. Writing *my love, my home* with pulsing lights, toward a remote nothingness. *Give me time and courage to wait, even though I don't know what for.* Courage and waiting in my hands. *I know my hands better than I know my face . . . Those who think that our hands belong to us are wrong; we belong to our hands.*

What was I thinking about while I watched the documentary? As I cried through almost all of the second half, after the mother's death, I thought I understood. That it was speaking to my sensibility and that I could come to truly love the person who'd sent that film to me, the person whose sensibility it also spoke to. A horse with the tail of a fish. The memories we must create together so that the emotions make sense.

Perhaps when she returns, I can tell her: "Every day when you were with her and not writing to me, I watched the documentary until I saw the whole thing. So its delicacy and tenderness left no room for bad thoughts. If we are capable of feeling such beauty, we must be capable of making it ours." *That which human beings cannot explain, they invent. I no longer know what it was like to talk to you, or what it's like to have a mother.*

Allowing life through, accepting, taking desire with all the contradictions it provokes in me. Accepting—isn't that what I'm doing? Light enters through the picture windows in the living room and undresses the furniture's soft wood. If I step into the light, it is she who is on top of me, dazzling and blurring the edges of my right foot. I am sitting in an armchair the color of dark jade that in turn rests beside two other empty green armchairs. The house number is three, a number that aspires to an ideal or a tendency to triangulate everything. While some people try to make things *square* up or perfectly *round* them out, the owner of this triangular house supports the world on three legs. A house built for three? Her, the dog, and me. Greta, me, her. How can three be satisfying for us? A number that sets out the possibility of a relationship in two directions, but at the same time preserves our solitude, keeps it intact.

With three, there is always one who is alone. There is always a moment when one watches while two live. The gaze is privileged because it captures the beauty and intimacy from a distance so short that it would be impossible to have such perspective any other way. What is the flip side of that privilege? The strangeness of being inside and outside at the same time. Of existing and not existing for the others.

An invented memory:

We've spent the day together, and she who does not live at the house says goodbye. The image of Greta entering the writer's mouth, who leans on the sideboard right by the front door, where mail, keys, shells and pebbles from the beach accumulate. It is a slow goodbye. I see Greta's movement, but not the writer's. I wonder if she also moves forward, or if her tongue simply rests and her lips open as she accepts Greta passively.

I wait for the moment to end. Perhaps I feel curiosity or I'm faking it, because I'd want to be more curious than annoyed by jealousy. But we are more our passions than our projects, the latter being a mere intention that has yet to materialize.

Two kiss each other, one watches. And the one who watches, where should she rest her eyes? On the floor, on her phone screen? Or right smack on their two bodies as if there was nothing wrong in holding that image? How long does the kiss last for the one who is observing it? Much, much longer than it does for the two who are kissing each other.

Because I am one of three, I know the frustrated transitoriness of the ghost who enters houses and crosses through rooms where the living eat, defecate, make love.

Then Greta kisses me. And my kiss doesn't exist, since inevitably all my attention is focused on establishing a pessimistic comparison where I imagine I come out losing: fewer seconds, less desire, less depth. She prefers to kiss the writer over kissing me. Is that true or my insecure imagining? It's impossible to know what is fair and real; partial and anxious experience is our only witness. I don't know if Greta chooses me or takes me simply because she found me there, in the middle. Some sort of appendage that grew out of what she desires and that is not me. I don't know if the writer is slowly coming nearer or drifting away, in this exasperating slowness through which we relate to each other.

If only they didn't exist. If I'd never met them.

I have to force myself to forget the morning with Greta. All her gestures of affection and generosity. She is not my enemy. The good things that happen to us are also real, I tell myself, not only the bad ones.

I go to the cloth bag where I keep my underwear and look at two recently developed photographs: she and I in summer robes, her hand on my belly and her lips on the fabric at the height of my breastbone. The gesture is tender; she isn't looking at the camera I hold up. How could she have been so sweet so soon?

I have a shitty night. Dawn comes again.

Alone in the house I am the guardian of the base. The one of a three where two spend the morning on another beach that is not this one, the afternoon reading in cozy restaurants, tasting several local wines before deciding on a bottle, pointing with an index finger resting on the menu: bread smeared with tomato, garlic, and oil; olives and scallops that arrive to the table on small plates no bigger than an open palm. For dessert, a crunchy croissant with melted chocolate that stains their mouths, fingers, and chins. Admiring the artistic woodwork of art-nouveau shelves that display different types of liquor. Ending the night with one from Minorca. Talking about an island, about returning together to the island where Greta's family still lives.

But listen to me, Greta. I want to go there, too. Would that be possible, or would it break the tacit rules of the game? The ones that are perhaps familiar to you two, but that I, of course, don't know because time's passed and I haven't heard anything from you. Can I travel with you? Would you want that? Could that even be a remote option? That some other day you would come pick me up in your car with your wide, clean smile and your sunglasses perched on your head? Because you love sunglasses even though you barely need them. You, who have the darkest eyes I've ever seen (and, because you don't worry, it doesn't seem you are run through with dark passions, insecurity, and envy), can look straight at the sun.

I would've liked to have told you that I missed making love like that, in the morning, dawn breaking beside such an alert, awake body. Because the morning follows the night and I've always felt that nights of desire are exhausting, alcohol filling our memories with wisps of fog, and that is when dawn surprises us, awakening beside someone who hasn't always been there.

One moves first and the other is still, waiting. The camera was on the bedside table, also placed for you to take it. I think you wanted light to enter the room, but just a little bit, enough to draw the bedspread, the thighs spread in sleep, the outline of who was there with you. You tried various positions. I could recognize the sound of your movements; with closed eyes I imagined you pushing the curtain's two tongues toward different heights, leading a ray onto me like playing with the sun and a mirror.

Then a silence, the silence of your gaze behind the camera, followed by the mechanical sound of the shutter: a wide, curt, very characteristic sound.

You could have all of this, Greta; it was for you: the room, the morning, the nakedness. Your attention made me softer and curvier.

✦ ✦ ✦ ✦

Beauty can be held without wilting when it is one of us who discovers it, inaugurates it with aesthetic attention, like an act of creation and re-creation anew. The other, imagining as well, surrenders to a possibility that exists since long before we arrived there in that overtaken house together. The story that links us with this magnetism is new, like a lamb opening its eyes after leaving the placenta behind, but also ancient; it is in museums and dictionaries of mythology, where Leda is seduced by a god converted into a swan, who knows that, in order to bed the virtuous woman, he must offer something other than a male body.

This is what the swan offered: a chest of white feathers and the wingspan to hold up lovely Leda while he penetrates her. Who doesn't dream of being weightless at some point? Nestled on the bedspread or pulled by a river's non-negotiable current. In the thrust of a pushing animal who is us. Capable of opening one up, capable of opening up legs, hindquarters, for one another.

I remember us. Sitting with you at my back and you wrapping your arms around me, quickly, present in everything sensitive. Then my nape leaning back, and that was the surrender: not measuring proportions, hungry for what you wanted or were willing to give me. Being open—open mouth, open will—rounded and juicy corners.

The writer sends me an image of the sea, a grayer one than we usually see in the mornings, with some large sailboats cruising through the background. Her message says: *Bon dia: so similar and so different. I'll be back tonight. Why don't you take some fish broth out of the freezer, and we'll make a warm soup with noodles?*

So similar and so different. The sea? Or spending her days with Greta versus spending them with me? If at least she'd written *Looking forward to seeing you*, that would have been enough for me, but I don't know what that message would mean to Greta. A betrayal of their time shared? Perhaps not for her, so loving and joyful; just for me, a maniac who twists everything around and is suspicious of everything.

I wish I could feel light. Maybe only those who have been loved enough travel lightly. Those who have been, at least once, the favorites.

I could leave. That would be a display of character for the first time. It would break the diamond thread that keeps me tied to this space, that keeps me tied to *her*. But, really, it would be a false gesture of intention that would work against a deeper desire: to remain here waiting for things to turn my way.

The house becomes dense as petroleum, sticky, with grippy surfaces. Then it turns smooth, with cutting shapes and a sucking void. I stay still, standing by the front door, staring at it but not trying to open it. My body is not responding; only my mind moves rapidly, linking thoughts without my having control over them. Something inside accelerated excessively—the messages suggesting running away mix with strategic thoughts, which calculate the possibilities that, if the writer returns and finds me in her house, if I thaw the broth and wait to have dinner with her, perhaps tonight something I desire will happen.

12.

Notebook

And I had to hold her hand through the entire dinner because I saw the fear in her eyes, the cesspit of dark emotions accumulated over the weekend. From her face, which tried to follow the conversation but showed blocked expressions that didn't trace their full path, I understood what she'd been imagining, alone in the house.

I held her hand and spoke softly to her all night long, because what did it matter that reality hadn't been like her nightmare if in the end she had experienced total agony through her imagination? I thought about saying that to her: *It's not what you are imagining. My relationship with Greta has no sex or any falling in love. Yes, I like to look at her. Her beauty accompanies me; we accompany each other in life, nothing more.*

But I wouldn't have been able to tell her that without a wave of resentment forcing me to reproach her: *You are so afraid because you've thought I am like you, that I have the same needs and that I've responded in the same way you did, impatient and angry, because love did not unfold at your pace. Insecure and defeatist, it is you, you, you, Photographer Girl, who has sought out an escape from a path toward seduction that you find claustrophobic, so much so that it makes you doubt me, but most of all, it makes you doubt yourself.*

At some point she let go of my hand, stood up nervously from the chair, saying she had to peel some tomatoes she'd cooked. I was telling her about a birdwatching spot in the Ebro Delta, and she was nervously glancing around in every direction. She didn't want to believe that my interest in the Tancada lagoon was the real subject, and she was growing impatient for the definitive topic to be broached. She unbuttoned her shirt sleeves and rolled them up to her elbows so she could remove the thin skin from the tomatoes, focusing her stare on them. I know I could have said something then that would have clarified the situation, but the pain kept me silent. What right did I have to tell her that her dealings with Greta had shattered the fantasy I'd had for the two of us? The longing for something simple that was slowly developing on firm ground. And what right did I have to desire from others, once again, something so similar to traditional love, to the ideal of loyalty we were raised with?

And that was how I spent a weekend on Greta's arm, visiting rice fields and sucking the delicious heads of horrible mantis shrimp. Looking at the line of her thighs beneath her pajama pants, not out of a desire for her but to imagine how she would look at the photographer. Being her friend, wanting to be her friend, nodding with patient complicity during her telling of the story of their romance, shaking my head when she asked me, "You don't think it was wrong, do you?" Half tormented, incapable of opposing her, incapable of letting myself be the jealous and possessive older woman who, nevertheless, in some regards, I've been my whole life.

A territorial woman, who needs to have a certain amount of control over the space of her house where the girl is now, the girl I can no longer imagine as *my girl* for even a second, while I'm invaded by unpleasant thoughts that sound like some old bolero: *It can't be anymore. If we make love tonight, the images of lovemaking with the other woman will still be too fresh in your mind. Perhaps you'll close your eyes while you kiss me and think of her*. What does it matter? I've already entered into this state of insecurity, in the crisis that drags me to a kind of discourse that in other moods I would have considered unbearable. One tomato, another tomato, a mountain of torn red skins on one corner of the wooden board. Wide-fingered hands holding the knife. Peeling like someone plucking a bird. An image that implies handiwork or violence. It's unclear.

The lack, the need for a body and a passion that shatters the limits of my life continues stalking me now with the same force it had when I was sixteen. But unlike before, I no longer believe it's fair to vent that kind of fervor onto others.

That is why I don't stand up and interrupt her absurd activity with my shouting. That is why I don't cry; I don't ask her questions.

Like the sun.
Like the foam hanging from the mouths of oxen.
Like a body locked in its borders, a body that has chosen
an unfair life for itself.

But what choice was there really? Perhaps I misinterpreted her signs, took the thought too seriously. What is she lacking in me?

If she had just taken my hand, instead of photographing it. If she had suddenly brought it to her sex and to her mouth. If that were her urgency.

The photographer speaks today at breakfast in faltering sentences as she smears rye toast with butter. She holds it up close to her mouth for a long time but doesn't bite it. She talks about her mother, who would often give her the silent treatment when she felt her daughter had done something wrong. "Since then I don't think I've been able to see anything positive in silence. It suggests someone is unhappy, or absent." I understand that my silence worries her.

A girl is punished with the silence of her mother. Not speaking to her is suspending her world. The power of not speaking: the exercise of authority that slowly shapes a small, anxious body.

The body that retracts attention positions itself in a place of violent, strategic power over the other who waits—her present suspended in torment—for the possibility of conversation bringing functionality back to her life.

And my silence, which is not intended as punishment but is merely a lump in the sternum. How can I explain it to her?

The silence of a blind eagle
who flies over the valley oblivious
to the state and form of things.

Even still, it is able to feed,
stay its course,
which is increasingly strange to others and to itself.

I've devoted all my life's energy to this sort of love . . . Would I be happier surrounded by daughters who fed off me? By others, still irrational, who imposed their need with innocent passion? To be able to forgive and love their violence. Two girls whose hair I would brush in the mornings and whom I would bathe in hot water at night. Their voices questioning me all day long, stealing my time, making me exist since I no longer have energy to think about my identity. But no one should prescribe motherhood to themself, creating life in order to make their own livable. All my love is not reason enough to bring another body into the possibility of anguish.

13.

A Strange Intimacy

We've been living in a strange intimacy for a few days now. At some point it happened—we found ourselves almost dirty and disheveled, living together, a different image, me occupying the house by acquired right. We looked at each other obliquely, but right into the eyes. It's a familiar place; we know each other in pain.

As we walked, she talked and gesticulated lightly. Suddenly a bramble hooked her for a few seconds as she passed and scratched her hand. I could see it in slow motion, a thorn cutting her index finger, a centimeter below the knuckle. A thin trickle of blood appeared immediately, and then settled into a small, curved red line on her svelte hand. The red stood out on her tanned skin, beside the gold rings.

I was quick and took a photograph just as the blood was beginning to dry. That hand could be the author photo for her next book. A portrait with no face capable of sating any expectations.

✦ ✦ ✦ ✦

The fizzy mineral water truck arrives once a week, and the writer receives it as if it were a visit she'd been awaiting for months. She peers through the kitchen window to make sure she's correctly recognized the sound of the small yellow-orange-and-blue truck's engine. Then, with a satisfied smile, she lifts up a plastic crate filled with empty bottles and sprints outside to exchange the empties for full ones. She briefly chats with the driver. Today she returns with a white envelope of thick paper, framed in an ultramarine blue band.

"The water access voucher. Every month they give us a free visit to the Vichy spa. This one's for you. I can go with you or . . . you can take a friend. Whatever you prefer, of course."

"Let's go together."

The writer listens to music, lying on the sofa, with the dog stretched out alongside her, snout hidden in her neck and hindquarters almost crushing her. She has a book she isn't reading resting on her lap.

"Have you ever heard Maria Arnal live in concert? I was thinking about the number three. Its inevitable repetition and also the possibility of overcoming the anxiety of number three by multiplying . . . That night someone took me to a concert . . . We were two people linked by a woman who sings. Maria was singing 'Com un meteorit lluminós, creuo el cel . . . ' *Like a luminous meteorite, I cross the sky* . . . and the woman I was with kissed me.

It seemed that on that night, for the first time, she was kissing me 'for real.' By 'for real' I mean with surrender, a certain kind of surrender. Of course she wasn't just kissing me, but also the music and Maria, celestial like a sphere in a white bonfire, burning blasts onto the stage. In a relationship, rarely are two people ever really alone."

"So our relationship is normal then?" I ask her.

We smile.

Something's happened. We are talking, fluidly, in no rush.

My voice blends with hers. We both increasingly resemble a third person, a mix of the two of us.

I left love twice. The first time was with my mother; as we sustained the pulse of our bond, she tired out and died. I had to leave. The second time was that relationship it seemed I'd be in forever. For seven years we were one of those modern couples. There was no need to place boundaries. In that way each of us suffered the freedom of the other. An ulcer-causing freedom we weren't prepared for. The sight of the other being truly free horrified us, even though we wanted to see each other with the eyes of friendship and not the eyes of a landowner witnessing their land being looted. The intention, wanting to be open, not wanting to be jealous or possessive . . . that intention only served to overexpose us. Traumatize us.

◆ ◆ ◆ ◆

Did you know I've always thought it's lovely to watch you eat? I love how you bite off pieces that are too big; you don't use silverware, and suddenly everything collects in your mouth. I've often fantasized with that image. The clumsy, hungry way you treat food. What you could one day do with me.

"I've never known my size, ever since I was a teenager. Depending on my mood, I would buy either a size 38, a 40, an XXL. I couldn't stand my outline showing the curves of my hips, thighs, or chest. I envied girls who were flat as a board. With long legs and no thighs, just a tiny little butt at the end. Later I desired women with heavy tits and generous thighs, but I knew I couldn't stand being one of them. I couldn't bear being looked at that way all the time. Like when I went out with no bra on under a too-thin T-shirt and realized the expressions on the faces of older men. The way their eyes were riveted on my chest and then their lips spasmed, and when they finally looked me in the face, it was with a violently contemptuous expression, as if my face didn't fit with their expectations—my bushy eyebrows nearly meeting over my nose, my dark, thick lips with a shadow of hair around them. My gray gaze. Pearl gray and sometimes red, fire, irritated.

"It wasn't the others' desire that shocked me, but the contempt that seemed to be attached to it, perpetually."

When, as a high schooler, a boy I liked stuck his fingers inside me, the following week the whole city knew about it. He didn't care about humiliating me, disrespecting me, because I was worthless. No one censored him for disclosing my private affairs. I had already been assigned the role of the monster, something excessive, desirous, and dirty. But nothing other than a hand has ever been able to touch me. My first political consciousness was that: an emphatic no to the rite of passage by which girls became women in that small city.

"Accepting that passion brings disorder, but to that extent?

"I fell in love with my best friend, who was very slender, and I started throwing up.

"Now there is always reflux and stomach pain. Do you think it's because of that? It wasn't a very long period . . .

"Look, what I have is often a feeling of constant inflammation on my right side, just below my lower ribs, that radiates out toward my back."

Nevertheless, I served my mother with labors of love. As a little girl I learned that a single face, like God, filled everything. I was attentive to any slight change in that face, which for me foresaw the state of the world. Sometimes, in a matter of minutes, it shifted from affection to rage. I learned to trace every little sign, contraction, change of expression. Anticipating, I would use my behavior to try to intervene, avoid the anger, or achieve even more recognition when something I did pleased her. The course of my life on a face.

The power of her expression subdued me and frightened me. Seeing it die would perhaps leave me frightened forever, which is why I avoided it. And your mamá? Did she have that face? The face of those who disappear. Didn't it scare you to see her like that?

"Only before looking was I scared. In the farewell, in the last loving gaze, horror does not exist, it has no place. The horrible images are created by distance; they are mental images.

"Perhaps you are too prudent. In general."

I don't follow a script or a life project. I am loyal to what happens in the body: If I feel love, I am prepared to surrender myself—to the wound, to the risk of loss. To sex and to the possibility of beauty. To the responsibility of beauty. To forever caring for a bird, a dog, a lover, or a daughter. Sharing body and touch are all that's needed to expose me to love transpiring.

Seduction is a path, one that not everyone takes, from radical difference to a desired familiarity. I wanted for us that seduction that doesn't consume the other, but rather opens up a house, a third space for two. But seduction is slow, you didn't understand that . . .

"I now understand what you are seeking, but I'm not sure it can be done with the same level of ambiguity as before. You could have told me that yes, there was desire, but that you simply needed some time to verify that I hadn't come to loot your home, to steal your image. Any waffling makes me feel very insecure; detours lead me to negative thoughts. I almost always interpret ambiguity as rejection."

◆ ◆ ◆ ◆

What you are saying sounds sweet. I never thought it could be sweet, that desire could be confessed without that entailing some loss of its power . . . its enigmatic power.

"What's difficult is having the strength to communicate it. More than the tension of the enigma you enjoy so much, I find something breathtaking in the reciprocity . . ."

That there is your hand. Your strong photographer girl hand that holds the weight of the camera steadily. That rounded index finger with its short nail that presses the shutter. At some point it will be inside me, along with this other finger. For the moment it is just your hand, which I've been observing for many days now. It has carried out all sorts of gestures, naked, before my eyes. There is something fabulous in the nature of a sexual organ that is always uncovered. Whose presence is central in the conversation, who addresses us, speaks to us with no shame.

14.

In the morning the breeze touches the folded sails of the ships on Altafulla's beach and makes them flutter. The catamarans went out to sea at first wind and lay on the sand for the rest of the day. The writer woke up early, went for a walk, and came back with a package of freshly ground coffee and a basket of small fish for frying.

"Get up, grab your camera, come on," she urged, peeking in through the door and resting the basket on the ground. I was still in pajamas, and I slipped on some sandals, covered myself in a cardigan sweater she'd left folded on the armchair, and followed her somewhat clumsily. We went down to the mouth of the Gaià River.

"Here, with the water in the background, this'll work. Take a photograph now."

She posed calmly. I caressed her with my eye, through the fine glass membrane. She seemed happy.

◆ ◆ ◆ ◆

Leaning on my legs, on the sofa, she reads me *Blue Eyes, Black Hair* by Marguerite Duras. It is a dense and enigmatic tale of oneiric theatricality. Someone, suffering from melancholy, asks a woman to sleep with him in an apartment by the sea. Over many nights he observes her, but he never resolves to touch her. The writer reads for almost two whole hours before we go to sleep. Every so often she stops, comments on a phrase, makes sure I'm still awake.

It was on the highway at sunrise, after the second café had closed, that he said he was looking for a young woman to sleep with him for a while, because he was afraid of going out of his mind.

The bed is too soft, and at the bottom of my back I feel I'm sinking and my spine is curving. To one side, the dog sleeps with her snout near my mouth, so I can smell her strong animal breath. The fur on her neck, where I sometimes bury my nose, doesn't smell of dog but of her friend's perfume. Talcum powder, sweet fig milk, hand soap. I nuzzle my face there while I stroke her ears, flattening them, tilting them back. Placid and slow, the dog surrenders to my hand.

Suddenly, she hears the door to the writer's bedroom open and she leaps out of our nest, rushes toward the hall where we can already hear her footsteps approaching. I recognize them by their reverberation, her gentle tread.

"Good morning, babe." She is looking toward the empty space between my sheets. Then she asks, "Do you think it's wrong to be jealous of a dog?"

She smiles at the edge of the bed like a little girl asking for permission. She slips inside.

Sara Torres is a Spanish poet and novelist. In 2014, she won the Gloria Fuertes Poetry Prize. For her first novel, *Lo que hay* (*X Is Where I Am*), she received the Javier Morote Prize, awarded by the Spanish Confederation of Booksellers' Guilds and Associations for the best new author in 2022. She holds a PhD, specializing in theories of lesbian queer desire and fetish.